THROUGH THE ASHES

BOOK 1
SWORD OF FIRE

J.A. Culican

Edited by: Cassidy Taylor

Cover Art by: Rebecca Frank

ISBN-13: 978-1719205931
ISBN-10: 1719205930

www.dragonrealmpress.com

For Fiona.

CONTENTS

Bells struggled to push the big wheelbarrow across the muddy, churned earth. Smoke from the little village, which was still burning, stung her eyes and lungs. Humans had recently started building their homes from plastics which released a horrid, acrid scent. To her friend, Crys, she said, "I still wonder how humans survived for so long after wrecking the planet."

"At the moment," Crys replied, "I'm more concerned about getting our work done without breaking anything or giving the foreman some other excuse to cut our food rations."

Well, humans might now have been reaping what they sowed—it was their ravaging the planet that had led to the Pures coming back into the world, to the humans' misfortune—but the elves' burning of humanity's plastic cities and villages wasn't doing the damaged Earth any favors. "I think the White King cares more about other things than about the environment. After all, how long ago did the Pures leave humans to their misery the last time? Three thousand years? Six thousand?"

"Watch what you say, Bells. But it was long before my time, anyway," Crys replied and then grunted with the effort of keeping the wagon upright.

Bells glanced at the nearby "punishment pit," a mound of neatly-laid human bodies that had completely overflowed the original 8'x16' hole in the ground. That night, the elves were likely to cremate those remains; they were big on "purifying" through fire, despite the toxic fumes now pouring into the air in cities all over the world.

Oof! While she'd been looking at the horrible mound of the dead, her human-sized wheelbarrow caught its single front wheel in a rut and tipped over. It was far too large for Bells to catch in time. Crys cursed, then she and Bells frantically scrambled to pick up the fallen tools and seed packets. Thankfully, most had remained inside the wheelbarrow.

Once she'd picked up what she could, she furtively looked around. "I don't see the foreman." Hopefully, the elf hadn't seen her, either.

"He's probably passed out on the Other Side, though. Elves are way too fond of the humans' fermented drinks."

Bells shook her head at the thought, wishing she were also on the Other Side, and started pushing again. This time, she swore she'd pay more attention to where she guided the stupid, heavy contraption. "Wheelbarrows were a dumb design."

"They're meant for bigger creatures than we poor little fae who get stuck using them. The elves should have left some humans alive."

Though she was stuck using those tools for now, Bells reminded herself that the elves said they'd soon use the Earth's resources for good building implements their fae servants could use better—

A shadow passed overhead, and she looked up. A big flock of birds was darkening the sky, coming up from the south. The sun was in her eyes, so she raised one hand to shade them and tried to figure out what kind of birds they were.

Standing beside her, Crys said, "It's the wrong time of year for mass bird migrations."

Bells closed her eyes and let her senses carry outward, entwining with the natural energies of the area, the wind, the sky, the plants... "Oh no," she whispered hoarsely, "those aren't birds." No, they were huge, long, and vicious-looking.

"Dragons," Crys sent out an empathic, panicked cry to the other fae, who scrambled almost instantly into any handy hidey-spots. Fae were good at hiding, and their magic was perfect for that—as soon as they were in cover, they seemed almost to fuse with the rocks, the shadows, or whatever they were behind. It was a survival trait, useful since the other Pure races considered fae to be little better than humans.

The elves often talked about the vicious, arrogant dragons who thought they ruled the Pure races. Violent and brutal, the elves said. Three of them separated from the vast, dark cloud of wings. In the blink of an eye, they were streaking like meteors at the ground right toward her.

Bells looked around frantically; Crys was gone, but she couldn't see anywhere to hide.

Just before they hit the ground, the three spread their wings and set down hard enough for Bells to feel the impact through her slippered feet. She staggered backward, her task forgotten, and in a panic, she threw her arm up to protect herself. "Are... Are you going to eat me?"

The dragon in front, the biggest of them, with massively thick, red scales from snout to tail—much thicker than its two companions'—laughed, and that sound was terrifying. Its eyes never left her, looking her up and down and then gazing into her face. Probably deciding how best to prepare a fae meal. The other two were nearly as large as the red one, but with thinner scales. They looked in every direction and ignored her. Probably making sure their meal wouldn't be interrupted.

She scrambled away from them.

The dragon in front spoke in a growling voice that was hard to understand. "No, little fae, not unless *you* killed the humans who lived here." Even speaking in its dragon form, Bells could hear a hint of humor in its voice.

She felt a glimmer of hope, but also confusion. Why would *dragons*, masters of the Earth and sky, care about the lives of a few clever animals? So, she decided to ask. She might as well satisfy her curiosity before she died. "But why? Humans don't have souls. They're nothing to you. The elves say humans are little more than clever monkeys but much more violent and destructive."

She watched his reaction intently, studying the magnificent creature. It stretched at least fifty feet from snout to tail. Its heavy head was nearly as wide as its body, boasting sky-blue, reptilian eyes. Ridges rose from a point almost between its eyes, spreading out as they went back across the top of its head and behind its ears. Spikes grew from the ridges, getting longer and thicker the farther back along the crests they went.

The mighty dragon shook its head, snapping her out of her examination, and said, "The humans have souls. They are Pures, like us. They've just lost their way and abandoned their connection to the Great Creation. Sad, miserable, lonely things, even when they are wealthy and powerful, even when surrounded by friends. They grow old and die in a blink of the eye, and when they die, their souls—with all that accumulated wisdom and experience—are lost rather than rejoining the great cycle. They have no Spirit Pool."

Her jaw dropped. Humans once had a gift from the Great Creation, the source of all things? They had souls, like Pures, but no way of continuing the eternal cycle of rebirth? That made no sense. Surely the dragon could see how humans had treated the Earth while the Pures were gone.

"Well, *we* didn't kill them," she replied. "We fae just try not to get ourselves killed. Obey and work, that's what keeps us alive. Most of the time, at least. Sometimes, an elf or were gets bored and hunts us for sport or works us to death for entertainment, yet we fae survive."

"How do you manage?" the dragon asked, sounding... sad? Genuinely interested, at least.

"Any way we can," she replied. The dragon's seeming innocence was startling.

It bared its teeth at her, wickedly sharp in front with the broader teeth in the back, but it seemed amused more than angry. "I like you, little fae. What is your name? I am Jaekob, son of Mikah."

Bells pushed herself off the ground and got to her feet. She was terrified of this Pure, who looked like he could bite her in half and devour her in two gulps, but where could she run? Nowhere. All she could do was stand tall, so that's what she did. Chin up, gaze steady, heart pounding in her ears like a jackhammer, she said, "My name is Bells." Maybe it would be smarter to flatter it. She added, "Dragons are heroes in all the old legends. Are you here to help us?"

Jaekob's mouth turned down at the corners and looked away for a moment. Was he ashamed? Could a dragon feel disappointment? Maybe, because when he replied, he was practically mumbling. "No, we're not here to help. Not you, at least. I grew curious about you and this place as I flew over the village, that's all."

She felt her hope die. The dragons weren't here to save them. But at least they weren't coming up to eat her kind, either. She was no worse off than before. She struggled to force a smile onto her face.

The dragon smiled back, baring his fangs. His eyes roamed over her and she felt her cheeks flush. "Bells... A pretty name," he said, snapping her out of her thoughts, "and I'll remember your scent. If we meet again, you may not be able to tell the difference between one dragon or another, but I'll know you."

Well, she probably did smell. She'd been out in the fields working hard since yesterday without rest. She hoped that wasn't a threat when he said he'd know her and she wouldn't recognize him.

She decided to assume he meant it in a polite way, since it wouldn't do to upset such a huge, monster-sized Pure. The elves all said dragons ate Pures and humans alike, devouring whomever they wanted. She prayed her voice wouldn't crack and said, "You'll remember my smell? Sorry, I haven't bathed today. Too much work to do."

Jaekob let out his growling laughter again. Perhaps she'd get out of the encounter alive, after all. In fact, the dragon didn't seem at all like how the elves described them. It was confusing.

When Jaekob caught his breath, he said, "May we meet again, in this life or the next, little fae Bells."

Imagine that! A mighty dragon, remembering little ol' Bells. It was hardly believable. She smiled back, waving until the three lifted off the ground, beating their scary-big wings hard and creating a strong wind. She could only imagine the power it must have taken to lift their huge bulk off the ground.

Maybe they weren't back in the world to help the fae, but she suspected they might have something to say about the other Pures trying to take over the place. She smiled as she thought about angry dragons stacking elves in a pit, just as the elves had made her and the fae stack the ugly, helpless humans.

She only hoped she lived long enough to see that. If the foreman found out she'd talked to a dragon, he'd probably throw her on that stack himself. Time to work harder than ever to catch up, so the foreman had no reason to ask questions.

J.A. Culican

Ten years later...

The early morning light streaming through the window shutters woke Bells gently. For a moment, the new daylight's warmth and glow brought a smile to her face, and she stretched. The smile was short-lived, however. The list of all her daily chores came flooding to mind. The elf's inspection was coming, and any family that didn't pass... Well, she didn't want to think about that.

A quick glance told her that her sister, with whom she shared a bed, had already risen. Bells didn't hear anyone in the hut, so her sister was probably already out getting started on the day's work. She sat up and slid her feet off the bed to the packed earth floor and looked around, bleary-eyed.

The hut was a mere fifteen feet around, and the earthen walls were smooth and unadorned. Fae magic had raised it up quickly, but their overseers hadn't allowed any time for the usual decorations beloved by fae. It was a depressing, simple mud hut. The bed above hers belonged to her two brothers, and at the hut's far end was a larger bed for Mother and Father.

In the center, there was a fire pit rimmed with bricks, and a metal bar strung across the pit's length, standing on two metal uprights. From that hung every cast-iron pot and cooking utensil they owned. The remaining wall space was dedicated to storage for all the things they needed just to survive.

The bathroom was an outhouse, of course. No one in the village had been given enough time to create an inside bathroom.

She really wished the elves hadn't destroyed the human homes, as they'd had indoor plumbing and electric appliances. Her village's overseer, however, had said that low-born fae didn't deserve even a human house, and the buildings had all been burned, just like the bodies of all the people who had once lived there. Poor humans.

It occurred to her that she should save her pity for her own people, though. Why her family had let her sleep until dawn, she didn't know, but it was nice, even though it meant she had more work to do in less time.

She quickly got out of bed and donned her daily-wear dress. It was basically a woven-cloth sack with holes for her arms and head, and a belt around her waist to keep it in place, hold her pouches, and carry a couple of tools. She grabbed the last bit of flatbread in the frying pan over the pit and stuffed it in her mouth as she headed out the door.

Like every morning, her first chore was to fetch water for the family. From behind the house, she grabbed the yoke, a wooden beam with four 5-gallon buckets attached to it that was meant to rest on her shoulders. She threw it across her back and came around to the front.

Old Mr. Drumm was stooped over the little garden in front of his house, and he waved. She waved and favored him with a smile—he had been nice to her through the entire ten years the fae had been farming this land. His assigned garden was small, only a quarter-acre, but it was all his old bones could handle. It was sad that he no longer had a son to care for more land. The boy had been devoured by a werewolf two years ago, and not even for meat, but just for sport, as punishment. Fae were disposable. His household had the same burden to supply the elves as every other, but at least he only had to feed himself and his wife, and they were old and didn't eat much anymore.

Bells passed between several mounded dirt rows built over piles of chopped wood. Between the nutrients that provided and the little boost from fae magic, her family's farm was massively overloaded with food. They couldn't touch any of it since that food belonged to the elves, but it had kept her family safe from the sort of treatment Mr. Drumm and his family got. Twice during the first year, fae families had eaten some of the food the elves claimed. Mr.

Drumm's son was one of them. The "thieves" had been torn apart in the middle of the night, and their screams still haunted her sometimes in her dreams.

When she reached the nearby stream, she hooked her yoke up to the rope they had stretched across the water and wheeled her buckets out toward the center. She played out some rope, and the buckets dipped into the water, filling. Then, she hauled them back to the stream banks and settled her yoke back onto her shoulders. She gave a friendly nod to the other fae waiting for her to finish before fetching their own water.

Once she got back to the house, she poured her buckets into a large barrel. It had been empty, but after pouring in the fresh water, the lines told her that she had just over 17 gallons for her family to last the day. She scooped out a little bit of that water into a much smaller bucket, then headed toward the rows and rows of crops her family tended.

Father was already in the fields, sweating from the effort of brushing all the ashes off the crops. He saw her coming and smiled. "Plants can't get no sunlight if they're covered with ashes, you know."

Bells nodded. The mounds and all their plants had to be brushed off—with a little help from their magic—at least twice a day, or they would start to wilt. It sometimes seemed the whole world had a thin layer of ashes.

She filled the little scooper in the bucket with water and handed it to her father, who drank it down eagerly.

"So, what's on your agenda for the day?" Father asked as his hands moved deftly over the foliage, dislodging the ash. The aisles between the rows were all gray with a thicker layer of ash built up over the years they'd been there. Eventually, the ash and the chopped wood under the mounds would combine to make the soil fertile again, but much of their soil was still almost barren thanks to the disgusting chemical fertilizers humans had seemed to love so much. Didn't they know it killed all the useful bacteria and fungi in the soil? Father had once told her humans had known and just didn't care, so long as they made their "money."

She found that hard to believe—no society could outlive its soil.

Bells shook her head to clear her thoughts and smiled at Father. "I need to harvest a bunch of the herbs on the floating rafts on our fish ponds. Now that the fish aren't dying off so fast, the herbs we grow there are practically better than what we grow for the elves."

Father's eyes went wide and he pursed his lips. "Don't say such things, dear. You know they have ways of hearing us. By the White King, if they think we're holding out on them, it will go bad for us."

She nodded and looked away, unable to meet his eyes. She had just brought danger to her family without even thinking about it. She had to be more careful, as her sister had always been happy to tell her.

She made her way back to the stream and moved farther downstream. There, they had dug a long series of pits which connected to the stream at two points, allowing the water to flow in and then back out again. The fish needed oxygen, after all, and nothing was better than the aerated water from the stream.

She looked at her family's fish pit and smiled. It was deeper on one end than the other, sliding sharply upward before leveling out about a foot below the surface on the upstream end.

Half the pond was solidly choked with water plants—weeds, the humans had called them—and the other half belonged to the fish they raised. It had been easy to convince the plants to grow only on one side once Father had explained to them that they would get lots of nutrients from the fish. It was a symbiotic relationship. A couple times a year, the fae waded in with sickles and chopped down most of the plants, leaving the roots and some greenery. What they cut, they added to the soil in their gardens, greatly accelerating the soil's recovery from the sterilization of human fertilizers and insect control chemicals. Why humans didn't want insects in their gardens, she had no idea—they attracted snakes, lizards, and birds, all of whom enriched the soil with their droppings, attracting yet more animals.

The fae had only been in the village for a decade, but soon now the soil would begin to produce as much food as the humans ever had, so long as they allowed nature to balance itself.

Today, the fish seemed happy. A couple of them jumped into the air as she approached, and Bells smiled at their greeting, tossing in a couple handfuls of mealworms.

As Bells looked around, she saw that the raft gardens were growing rich and green. If the elves didn't take it, her family might actually eat well that winter after they jarred up whatever they didn't eat, smoke, or dehydrate.

Satisfied, she headed toward the woods to see if her two older brothers needed any help. Today, they were chopping wood. Other days, they might be hunting and hard to find, which was a pain. On the other hand, when they chopped wood, they needed water twice instead of just once.

"All things in balance, and balance in all things," she muttered to herself. Those were the words by which the fae lived.

She left what water remained in the bucket with her brothers so she could carry an armload of cut wood back to the hut, then layered that evenly on top of the curing stack on the hut's southern wall. The sunlight there helped to cure it faster—what little sunlight got through the smoke haze that still covered the Earth since the time of the great burning, when the Pures had stepped out of shadows to once again declare war on humankind.

Just as with every other war, there was no reason for the slaughter as far as she was concerned. So the humans had been destroying the Earth. Who cared? The Pures had lived in the Shadow World for a millennium, and she would have happily lived there forever. There was plenty of food to go around, and as long as the fae obeyed their betters, the elves, trolls and weres had pretty much left them alone.

Not so, here on Earth.

She headed into her family hut, deciding to spend the rest of the day at the loom and spindle, making fabric and thread for ropes. There was no end to the chores that needed doing, and even in a large family like hers, there were never enough hands to do it all. She began spinning thread from the many plant fibers her family collected whenever they could.

A loud bang at the front door made her jerk, dropping her thread spindle, and she jumped up to get the door. She had irritation written on her face. "I'm coming, hold your horses."

When she was halfway across the room, whoever was outside banged again, making the whole door shake in its frame. "By the White King, I said I'm coming!" she yelled.

She opened the door, but when she saw who stood there, she let out a little squeak and tried to close it in the thing's face. A huge, obsidian-colored hand slapped the door open almost like swatting at a bug, but the movement was powerful enough to send her flying. She landed on her back and looked through the doorway, eyes wide; she saw only a bulging belly and two stumpy legs.

He squatted down, looking through the doorway, and Bells squeaked again. The troll's face was narrow, all angles and corners, looking like he had been rough-hewn into some sort of pitch-black rock sprinkled with blood-red flakes. His nose was easily half a foot long and it curved forward like a hawk's beak. His eyes were just as predatory as any bird of prey's, despite taking up twice as much of his face as any human or fae eyes. The thing grinned and bared black, rotted teeth.

A troll.

"She's a tasty morsel, yes she is. It wonders how she tastes. Is her marrow delicious and bitter? If she has no answers, it gets to find out." The troll curled his lips back again in a snarl.

Bells froze in place, sitting up on her elbows and staring at the black and red-flaked eyes that peered back at her. "I... What answers? You shouldn't be here. The elves are supposed to inspect us today. If they find you poaching—"

The troll laughed, his belly shaking. It sounded like a pig snorting over and over again. He said, "Answers to questions, yes, of course. The elves aren't coming, not today." He clicked his teeth together over and over again at her and made a sucking sound through his teeth. Then he said, "She shows it where her fish are unless she wants to be the snack."

He reached one hand through the doorway. Impossibly long fingers, thin and bony with four-inch, talon-like claws, grabbed Bells around her ankle and dragged her outside.

Holding her upside down, he brought Bells up to his face. "She shows the fish, or she is the fish. Which does she want?"

Bells clasped both hands over her mouth, trying not to scream. If her brothers came back, they might be tempted to do something stupid. Then, her whole family would suffer. She nodded and said, "Yes, I'll show you the fish. We are doing well this month. Well enough that even a troll your size might get full on fish heads. Wouldn't you like that?"

The troll nodded frantically and cackled as he tossed her to the ground, letting her go. She landed in a crumpled heap.

She said, "Okay... Then let's... I'll show you where the fish are!" Staggering, she slowly rose to her feet, then she headed toward the stream and her family's fish pond. She silently prayed by the White King that her brothers wouldn't come out, not yet. They would definitely do or say something stupid to defend her, given how close their sister was to becoming a mincemeat pie. Trolls loved mincemeat pies.

She grabbed her shawl on the way out the door and said, "But our taxes aren't due until next week."

When she stepped outside, the troll didn't get out of her way. At 5 feet tall—average height, for a fae—she only came up to his waist. She was more than happy that his patchwork armor covered certain parts of him and had no desire to see any more of him.

"Your taxes are due when I say, little fae. Now, take it to the fishes." The troll bounced from one foot to the other in his excitement.

She led the monster through the raised garden beds in front of her hut and noticed that her father was suspiciously absent. He had just been there a few minutes before. Hopefully, he'd found a place to hide when the troll first approached the hut.

"Hurry up, girl," the troll said, sounding agitated.

When they got to the river, she led him to her family's fish pit. Right on cue, one of the fishes jumped into the air, making a splash when it hit the water again. The troll made a terrible noise that she took to be laughter. Maybe he was grinning, but with his protruding teeth, who could tell?

"This is my family's fish pond. We've got the population stable, so we should be able to meet the upcoming fish tax for the elves if you don't eat them all." She only hoped he was smart enough to figure out the hidden threat.

The troll grunted. "I don't care about elf taxes. I don't care about pop-loo-shins or big words from fae girls. Give me fish, or I find something else to eat." Again, he made the terrible huffing sound she took to be laughter.

Bells nodded. Better to be short a few fish than for her family to be short one daughter. "There's a fishing net right there. Just scoop it into the water and you'll get a fish. It might take a try or two, but it's not like the fish can run away." She shied away from the troll, trying to get out of the monster's striking distance. Trolls could get upset at surprising things, which she thought was because they were too stupid to understand and too big and mean to put up with feeling embarrassed.

She needn't have worried, however, because the troll jumped from a standing position all the way across the pond to where a round fishing net leaned against the family's supply bins. It snatched the net up in its long, gnarled fingers. Then, faster than she thought possible, the troll shoved the net into the water and dragged it halfway across the pond. When the net came dripping out of the water, it held at least four or five fish. Its thin webbing strained at the weight.

The troll reached out and propped up the net bottom with his other hand, shoving all four fish into his mouth at once. It began chomping, making happy little grunts while bits of goo and fish guts leaked out the corner of his mouth.

It was disgusting, but she forced a smile. "You like our fish?"

"No, fish are tasty snack... But, not enough in this pond... Where I find more fishes?"

Bells frowned. "I don't understand. This is all the fish I have. To get more fish, you'd have to go to a bigger fish pit, but those aren't my family's. And I know those fae have already paid their taxes."

Still holding the fishing net, he turned his back on her. "So? Show me bigger pond."

Bells felt a growing desperation. If she led him to one of the larger ponds, some other family might blame her for the loss of their fish, and her family couldn't afford to replace them. But she didn't want to think about what the troll might do if he got angry.

"I'm waiting," the troll snarled, taking a step toward her with his fists clenched.

Hastily, she said, "I told you, they already paid their taxes. No fish there. Understand? The elves took all their fish. They'll take ours when our taxes are due. Next week, remember?"

The troll spun around, lashing out with his fist, but she had wisely stayed out of range. The hand, as big as her head, whistled by with inches to spare. Startled, Bells fell over backward and scrambled away on her elbows as quickly as she could, eyes wide with fear.

The troll, seeing her reaction, began a full belly laugh, grabbing his stomach and bending over. The sounds reminded her of an angry wild hog. Trolls were vile, for sure. She scrambled back up to her feet and glanced around to find the best way to escape if the troll attacked her.

Catching its breath, the troll said, "Fine. No more fish. Not here for fish, anyway."

"Then what are you here for?" Then she hastily added, "Mr. Troll."

The monster grunted and shrugged his massive shoulders. "Here for weapon. Your fae family is making mace. Where is it? She takes it to the mace, or she is like the fishes."

Mace? What mace? Her family did have a little household smithy behind the hut. When had her family had been chosen to gather materials for and then build a troll-sized mace? No wonder Father had been so upset when he received the elves' latest "request" a few days earlier. It wasn't Father's habit to discuss such orders with his children, though.

She glanced up at the troll, risking upsetting him with accidental eye contact, but she needed to get a sense of his body language. He was shifting from foot to foot again, but this time, he didn't look happy-excited. He clenched and unclenched his fists and took a half-step toward her.

Hastily, Bells blurted, "Follow me. I didn't know we were supposed to make you a mace. I'm sorry I didn't know, but I do know where it would be. Our smithy is just behind our house. Come on, I'll lead you—"

The troll didn't wait for her to finish her sentence but turned and headed quickly toward the house, tearing up bushes and crops as he went. Thankfully, the fae did most of their agriculture by disguising plants as wild growth, making it harder for the elves to find it—and then tax it.

She ran to catch up, but the troll got farther ahead. She lost sight of him as he went around the hut to the back. She put her head down and sprinted as fast as she could.

When she got to the smithy, she found the troll on his hands and knees, peering through the fae-sized doorway. He had ripped the simple timber door off its hinges and thrown it twenty feet away.

"Where the mace? It doesn't see it. Fae girl, you go in and get it."

"Yes, sir," she said quickly and headed for the doorway.

After a quick glance around, Bells didn't spot the mace on the anvil where she had expected to find it, assuming her father really had been working on a commissioned mace. Her heart beat faster and the sweat she felt forming on her head wasn't only because of the fierce heat inside the smithy. Stepping farther inside, she said, "Are you sure the order went to *this* house? I think I would see a mace built for someone your size, sir."

Her life practically flashed before her eyes as she said it.

The troll outside paused for a moment and simply stared at her. She couldn't look away from the huge, monstrous eyes that held her riveted in place. Slowly, as though talking to an idiot, the troll said, "This is the house. *You* make the mace. Make it in the shop. You're in the shop. Or maybe you should find the mace before it thinks you are stealing. It counts to ten, then it eats you. One. Four. Two..."

Bells was in a panic, looking for the mace again, checking under tables, up in the rafters, even in small parts-bins. She was out of places to look but she wasn't yet ready to be eaten by a troll, so she ignored his noises of impatience outside the door and kept searching. Every time she looked somewhere and didn't find it, she let out a little panicked squeak she was hardly even aware of.

The troll's face disappeared from the doorway. Some wild, foolish part of her hoped the troll was going away. A moment later, she was brought crashing back into reality when he shoved his arm through the doorway, knocking over the anvil as though it were a paperweight. He didn't even flinch from the coals which landed on his hand and sizzled—his calloused hide was far too thick to feel such minor irritations.

In an instant, his fat fingers wrapped around Bells like thick, coiled ropes and yanked her out through the door at a dizzying speed. Bells screamed. In fact, she couldn't stop screaming. The troll cocked his head to one side and simply stared at her, his mouth twitching in what might have been an amused smile. When nothing happened, though, her screams eventually died on her lips, trailing away to nothing.

The troll suddenly burst into deep laughter, his whole body shaking, rattling her like a can of paint. She thought the beast might crush her, he squeezed so hard, but when he caught his breath, he relaxed his grip.

He dangled Bells only a couple feet from his face so he could look her in the eyes. "Well, you tell me why it not eat her now. Maybe it lets her live?"

Trying to find words, her mouth opened and closed, opened and closed. But when the troll made that expression again, the one he did right before laughing the last time, she found herself blurting, "If you eat me, I can't make sure we find your mace."

Bells and the troll both stood motionless, staring into one another's eyes, the troll looking confused and Bells too terrified to move, much less to say anything else.

At last, the troll nodded as he rose to his feet, the ground rushing away from her as he kept her held up to his face. "Fine." Then he simply opened his hand.

Bells fell to the ground, landing on her backside painfully. She let out a gasp of pain, and the troll made the huffing, chuckling noise again. Then he said, "Yes, fine. She gets the mace, it doesn't eat her.

If she steals its mace, her whole family is dinner. Har, har. Yum."

Bells nodded, her head going up and down like a bobble-head doll. "Yes, I swear, I'll find it. Come back next month and we'll make sure it's done."

She had barely finished speaking when the troll snapped, "No. No waiting. It comes in one week with the elves for getting taxes. If she has no mace, she leaves the village in its belly." His eyes glittered with mirth as he laughed at his own joke.

Bells didn't think it was so funny. She quickly agreed, then watched the troll's back receding as it strode away. From somewhere, surprisingly, an angry spark flared up in her heart. She could feel it growing hotter and hotter as the spark turned into an inferno. The most maddening thing about it was that there was nothing one little fae girl could do about it. Fists clenched, she stormed from the smithy to the gardens, kicking rocks as she went to find her father.

She found him on his hands and knees, hiding under a long, berry-laden branch. When he saw her, he blinked quickly and began moving his hands around the branch, picking fruit, then glanced at her. He did a double-take, pretending to be surprised. "Bells, how nice to see you. Is it lunchtime?"

She glared, crossing her arms and tapping a foot. "You don't have a basket. An interesting way to pick fruit, hmmm?"

"Oh. Well, my addled old brain must be going out on me. So... No lunch?"

"Father! Why didn't you tell me we got a ticket to make a mace for a troll? You didn't even have me go to the market to get more iron. That will use up every scrap we have and more, and you didn't even finish it. What did you think was going to happen? That troll almost ate me, and you knew it was coming. It's coming back for us all, by the way."

The old man's face flushed red in his cheeks, and lines appeared on his forehead as he furrowed his brow. "I'm sorry, Bells. What were we supposed to do? We simply can't afford to buy more metal. And you don't see a mace in the blacksmith shop because... Well, because I never finished it. We ran out of iron before I got halfway through forging the mace head. I don't know what to do." He put his face in his hands.

As Bells watched her father's expression go from embarrassed to frustrated to desperate, she felt the heat fading from the angry coal in her chest. Yes, he should have told the family about this, but she could hardly fault him for not having a mace ready when the despicable Pures didn't even bring the supplies needed for their orders.

At last, she let out a deep, frustrated breath, feeling sadness wash over her. "I don't know what we should do, either. We can't even borrow it from a neighbor." The fae helped each other because it was the only way to survive under the horrible elves and their cronies, but all their neighbors had been taxed almost to starvation, just like them. There was no way anyone in their village could keep up with the dues the Pures demanded.

Her father said, "I would dearly love to just pick up the whole family and move up into the Alps, but—"

"—but they'd hunt us down and kill us if we tried," Bells finished for him.

He nodded and looked away, unable to meet her gaze.

"Think about what we have to do," she said. "The troll said he'd come back with the elves when they come for our taxes next week. If I thought it would help, I'd just offer myself up for the troll's dinner, like your sister did, but I don't think that's going to do it. He said he'd eat our whole family unless we finish his mace."

Before he could respond, she spun on her heels and walked away, trying to keep her eyes from welling over in front of Father. She was just so overwhelmed. What could they do? She loved her family, but there was nothing any of them could do. The fae were considered second-rate Pures, at best.

She walked beyond the house, beyond the blacksmithing shed out back, and kept going. She looked down at her feet as she took one step after another, walking slowly to nowhere as her mind raced.

Then, a single thought struck her. Jaekob, that impressive dragon warrior she had met when the dragons rose back into the world of humans. They were practically invincible. Only they could help her and her family. Yet, they seemed content to keep the fae as their slaves. She had heard rumors of protests for equality, but they were just that—rumors.

Unfortunately, she knew the dragons weren't going to step in to help. Jaekob had said as much during their brief encounter.

Her thoughts raced in circles, going nowhere fast as she struggled to come up with another idea— something that would actually work—to save her family. She couldn't rely on anyone else, especially not the dragons.

J.A. Culican

Bells adjusted her backpack as she trudged along the cracked and broken road. It was her family's only real backpack, one of the strong ones made by the local human army long ago, back when the Earth was theirs. The humans made a lot of great backpacks for hiking and camping, but the hard part was finding one with no synthetic fibers. Those would, over the course of a few hours, give a fae cracked and bleeding skin.

The one she wore was made of canvas and coated with wax for waterproofing rather than the artificial garbage. Her father hadn't wanted her to take it, as it was one of their prized possessions, but the trip to the city was a long one. Simply carrying a sack over her shoulder would have rubbed her raw by the time she arrived. When he said no, she had smiled and nodded and then simply took it with her when she left late that night, along with what few trade goods she knew her family could spare.

The many thousands of the humans' horseless wagons—each weighing tons because they were made from metal that had been ripped from the Earth itself—had long ago been pushed off the road. The Pures had made the trolls do that work because the cars were just too heavy for their fae servants. The memory of trolls actually doing work brought a smile to her face.

She wiped the sweat from her forehead as she came to the crest of a low rise and peered down the other side at the outskirts of what had once been Philadelphia, a big human city. The Pures had spared it from total destruction, but only because the dragons had Risen before the other Pures got around to crushing it like they had so many other cities.

A man's voice behind her made her jump. "You aren't going down into that city, are you, sister?"

The words immediately calmed her racing heart. She turned slowly, a smile on her face, and saw another fae, a young man no more than two hundred years old, standing at the road's edge. His clothes were tattered but he was no worse off than most fae. He had no backpack or sack. A fae outside of his or her assigned territory had to be traveling on business, which meant he'd need a backpack, but since he had none, he had to have a camp nearby. She found herself looking for it.

The man chuckled. "Yes, sister, my family is camped just down the embankment behind that large rock. This close to the city, the roads can be dangerous."

Bells and the man stepped up to one another at the same time, both of them reaching up with their right hands to embrace the other fae's cheek, and touched foreheads. With the traditional Embrace of Unknown Family completed, she took a step back and smiled.

"Are you in need, brother?" she asked. Normally, she would have called him uncle because he looked a few years older, at least, but he had first greeted her with the friendlier title of "sister," establishing a relationship of equals. It was generous of him, and it meant he didn't intend to take anything of hers out of need.

She was happy, then, to offer from what little she had, but the man shook his head, eyes sparkling as he smiled at her generosity. "No, but thank you so much. I only came up to warn my sister about the dangers ahead. I wondered whether you had ever been into the city before and if you knew how to get around safely, down in that rat-hole of a city."

Bells felt her heart fall. How could a city with dragons be dangerous? Still, another fae had warned her, and in a friendly way. With her own inexperience, she'd just have to trust him. "But don't dragons rule city?"

The other fae laughed but his tone was good-natured. It didn't sound like he was mocking her, so she smiled back at him.

He said, "The dragons aren't here to save anyone, sister. Who on Earth would try to harm or steal from a dragon? No, their homes are safe. They turn a blind eye to the suffering around them since they don't have to worry about it personally. Remember, they only rose due to the humans. If they had known the Pures were behind the war above, they would have stayed below in their peaceful sanctuary."

Her heart fell even further. But then she thought about the time she had met Jaekob, a dragon. True, Jaekob said they weren't there to help anyone, but he didn't seem like the type to turn his back on his neighbors. After all, he had flown down to check on her and had been kind to her even though dragons ruled the Pures Council while fae like her served it.

Bells said, "What sort of dangers do dragons still allow to live in their city? I don't doubt you, but I find it confusing." She touched two fingers to her forehead, politely indicating that the confusion was due to her own stupidity rather than to the other fae being wrong or misleading.

He first pursed his lips, pausing a moment, then said, "For one, the city belongs to the Pures. Away from the city's center, many elves make their home in the rich houses of the humans who used to live there. Elves and dragons alike use trolls as guardians and werewolves as spies, assassins, and messengers. Trolls and werewolves are both just as prone to eat a lone, wandering fae as they are to leave her alone. But, you know, the Veil is torn now. Worse creatures than just cruel-hearted Pures have come into the world since then."

"Thanks," she said and frowned at the thought of having to face the city for the first time, but if she couldn't trade her goods for at least ten pounds of iron and then get it home, her family wouldn't outlast the week. "For my family, I have to go in there and trade for metal. Philadelphia has more iron and steel in one place than nature ever created, and the humans who hoarded it are dead. I'll have to take my chances."

The man shook his head, touching his chin with two fingers—he needed to speak a warning but hated the words he would have to say. She braced herself for whatever shock was coming.

"Sister, I respect you and your ancestors. Still, words must be spoken that don't sit well in my heart." He paused long enough for her to nod at him to continue. "There are still humans in Philadelphia. Now, they live scattered around the outskirts of the city or in tunnels beneath it. Abandoned buildings. Unused sewers. These kinds of places are now their homes. At least for the ones who survived this long."

"It doesn't sound like much of a way to live. Is there anything we can do to help them?" Jaekob had, shockingly, told her that humans were Pures, too, but that they had lost their connection to Creation. That had cost them whatever powers they must once have had. She didn't bother to tell the man because it was unbelievable. She wouldn't have believed it, either, if she hadn't heard it from a dragon's lips.

"No," the fae said, shaking his head, "it's not much of a life. But remember, in the best of times in all of human history, they nearly destroyed the whole planet with their greed, murdered each other by the millions, hoarded what they could, and cared nothing for their fellow humans, who starved. Since they've been slaughtered and forced to live in shadows, robbed of everything they considered their property, well... let's just say they haven't gotten much kinder since then. If you see a human, you can bet there's half a dozen more circling around behind you. Spot one, run. Your life will depend on that. And you know what they say about how humans view fae."

Bells shuddered. Humans had an unnatural attraction to fae. People said humans often took what they wanted, whether it was something or someone they desired. She definitely didn't want to meet any of them, as surprising as it was to hear that some still survived there. Philadelphia was the central Pures settlement in the entire region. Still, part of her was glad to hear there were living humans in the occupied areas. She never liked the idea that they were just rats that needed to be exterminated. Even rats served a purpose in this interconnected world.

"Thanks. I'll keep that in mind." She said farewell, then turned back to begin her descent into the city.

As Bells moved through the city's outskirts, she tried to sprint from shadow to shadow, staying in the dark as much as possible. Fortunately, it was late in the day and the shadows were long and getting longer. She was able to keep up her shadow-walk with hardly any effort. Although she didn't see any people, she could hear the sounds of activity all around. The buildings had crumbled for the most part. Most of the open areas were now in early succession forest, with saplings and bushes growing wild and rampant. Windows were broken. Streetlights were dark, most of them bent. Trash blew through the streets.

All in all, so much neglect and damage made it hard to imagine that anyone still lived there, even humans. Part of her hoped to see one, but mostly, well, she remembered what the fae on the road told her. She wasn't about to let her curiosity get her into the kind of trouble she couldn't get out of.

Although she was moving quickly and building up a sweat, her need to stay hidden meant she wasn't making good progress through the burned zone, or outskirts of the city. She desperately needed to be out of there by the time the sun went down. Even back at home, she had heard rumors of small packs of werewolves prowling the burned zones and the semi-rural areas outside the city for prey. Her parents had taught her that weres weren't bad—not even werewolves—but their hunting instinct was strong. They could only suppress it for so long and then their instincts took over. That's when they went fully wolf, and it was also when they were the most dangerous. No wonder the humans lived in the tunnels. Weres would never follow them down there. It had something to do with their sense of direction requiring the sun, the moon, or the stars. Underground, not used to relying on their other senses for direction, they feared getting lost. For the same reason, they hated entering buildings, too, unless they had cornered prey there and the building was small.

Her thoughts were interrupted when she heard a grinding sound up ahead. She slid into the closest shadow and hid with her shadow-walk fae ability. The noise grew louder and then the source came around the corner about a block away. Bells' jaw dropped at the sight.

It was a huge, horse-drawn wagon with three trolls marching in line on both sides and a fae sitting on the front bench to drive it. Most interestingly, though, she saw four humans sitting in the wagon. An elvish sign on the wagon's side proclaimed the humans had stolen food. It seemed odd the Pures would need so many trolls just to guard four humans, especially ones they'd bound at the wrists with ropes. The humans' clothes were mere rags, their hair long, and faces unshaven.

Seeing where they were headed, Bells' jaw dropped again. A few blocks down the road stood rows of gallows on both sides of the street. A few had skeletons hanging from rotting ropes. It was hard to believe those four people were going to be executed just for stealing food. No, actually, it wasn't so hard to believe. The elves were, after all, intent on exterminating humankind, and she knew from first-hand experience how the elves treated the fae, who were actual Pures. Humans were merely animals to the elves.

She shook her head and stayed hidden in shadows until the wagon passed, then slid around the corner into another shadow, and was gone.

Fortunately, she knew the First Councilor lived in the city and that Jaekob was his son, but the houses had numbers and the streets had signs, all written in human English. Frustrated at the sudden realization that she'd need the numbers and street name for Jaekob's house if she was to have any hope of finding him, she considered just going to the market, even though she knew Jaekob could help her family and the other fae in her village. She hadn't realized how large the city was since her only frame of reference was her little village and the small human town the elves burned to the ground during the first weeks of fighting. Philadelphia was vast. It probably stretched miles, unbelievably.

Well, she was a fae. Her kind couldn't just wander the city without their master's approval, so she decided just to go to the market where fae were allowed on their own. Surely someone there would know the information she needed and could tell her how to find the First Councilor's house.

Bells wove her hands in front of her face in an intricate pattern. Red and blue sparks and trails followed her hands, coalescing until they formed a simple glyph in the air. It began to drift, heading northeast. Bells smiled and with one flick of her hand, the glyph vanished. It was a simple spell to find the nearest large group of fae, useful for finding the nearest fae village if she were lost, but it worked just as well in Philadelphia—the market surely had the most fae in the city, after all.

A full hour later, she trudged into the market. It wasn't much to look at, really, just a few city blocks now burned to the ground. There were stone slabs— cement, she thought the humans called it—in neat rows throughout the market, dirt and grass sprouting between them.

Bells had a cousin, of sorts, named Hawking, one of the few fae allowed to live in the city. He was a merchant and had a stall in the Philadelphia market.

She shared a common grandfather with him. Though they had a different grandmother, family was family, blood was blood. All she had to do was find him. That turned out to be fairly easy when the third fae she asked gave her directions to his stall at the far end of the market.

When she found it, her eyes riveted onto the sign outside proclaiming its name, "Hawking General Wares." The play on words would have been amusing if she hadn't been so stunned by the shop itself—it was huge, previously a human house of considerable size. It sat right on the market's edge, the front porch part of the market's visible boundary. It was freshly painted—incredible!—in natural tones, with two men outside trying to wave people in. The store had a constant stream of fae, elves, and even trolls, all coming and going.

Even by elven standards, Hawking was doing quite well for himself. Maybe he could even help her with some useful supplies...

She made a beeline for the door, a double-door with glass panes amazingly still intact, and cautiously stepped inside. With one glance, she stopped in the doorway, stunned. The entire bottom floor had been hollowed out and now held rows of shelves stuffed with all sorts of goods, and the walls were lined with even more. Everywhere, every kind of Pure browsed the shelves.

A troll stood by the door wearing a crude uniform in the same colors as the building. He grunted at her, "In or out, fae. Yer blockin' the door."

How did her cousin afford a troll guard for his shop? It was incredible. Still stunned, she nodded and stepped aside to gawk some more. Just beyond the troll stood a low counter with two clerks who were haggling with customers. Along the wall behind them, where the troll could easily see, a stairwell led upstairs, but it was cordoned off by a velvet rope. That must be where Hawking lived, but Bells didn't see any way to get up undetected. Electric ceiling lights all over meant there were no shadows anywhere, so there was nowhere for her to shadow-walk.

Surely a merchant this large would have metal, but it wouldn't be on the shelves. She got into the line at the counter. When it was her turn for the first available clerk, she stepped up to face a young fae man wearing the same style of uniform as the troll guard.

"Welcome to Hawking General Wares, how may we serve you today?" His tone was flat and his eyes just slid over her, obviously a tedious greeting he gave a thousand times each day.

Bells smiled and said, "Yes, thanks, um... I need to buy iron, as much as I can carry, or as much as this will buy." She took off her backpack and set it on the counter. When she unzipped it, she showed the clerk her trade goods.

He nodded. "I'll have to weigh it to be sure, but it looks worth about twenty pounds of high-grade, or forty of the cheap stuff. It's melted down into small bars for ease of transport, our courtesy to our beloved clients. Is that acceptable?" The clerk picked up a quill and a pad of paper. He began tapping the quill tip on the paper, his lips pursed.

Bells had to think about it for a moment, so the impatient clerk would just have to wait. He'd offered more than she had figured her goods would buy. Melted down to bars, though, it would easily fit in her pack. But whatever she had told Father, buying metal was only part of her objective, and apparently, she could keep some of her trade goods to get around the city, if necessary.

At last, she said, "Ten of the high-grade and ten of the low-grade, please." As the clerk scribbled notes and then fished into her backpack, she bit her lip. It was now or never. Gathering her courage, she added, "Also, I'd love to see my cousin, Hawking. Can you let him know I'd like to talk to him?"

The clerk stopped writing and eyed her up and down. The slight wrinkle of his nose told her everything she needed to know about the urban fae's opinion of her. She was only a country fae, but she wouldn't have traded places with him for the world.

He pursed his lips. "And may I ask your name, and how you are related?"

Bells couldn't hold back her smile, despite the clerk's arrogant attitude. She might get to see her cousin after all. "Yes, my name is Bells. My father is Harp, and we're related by way of the same grandfather."

The clerk turned to the other one, an older woman, and handed her a slip of paper, whispering into her ear. She nodded once and headed up the stairs. Bells had the troll's full attention now, she realized, though he made no move toward her.

Five minutes later, the woman came back down. "Patron Hawking will see you now. Follow me." As she led Bells up the stairs, she looked over her shoulder and said, "I warn you, make no sudden movements. Do not touch him—ever. And try not to look him in his eyes. Do you understand?"

Bells nodded, a bit confused by the odd instructions. When they reached the top, the clerk led her down the walkway to the door farthest from the stairs, knocked twice, then opened the door wide. Bowing, she said, "Patron, your... relative is here. Is there anything else, sir?"

Bells stepped inside hesitantly. Why was she afraid? This was her cousin, after all.

"No," said a deep voice from the other side of a big, plush chair that faced away from the door toward an empty fireplace in the center of the room.

"Remember what I said," the clerk whispered, then closed the door behind her as she left.

Bells' voice spiked high with excitement as she said, "Cousin Hawking! I'm so glad to meet you, and thanks for taking the time to—"

The deep voice cut her off. "Yes, yes. Me too. Come, sit and tell me what this is about. I have little time, so make it quick, if you please."

She came around to the empty chair beside his—more lavish than anything she'd ever sat in—and smiled. He smiled back but it didn't reach his eyes. Eyes she was instructed not to look in, but it was too late. The only thing she saw there, though, was weariness, nothing scary, and Hawking didn't seem angry by it. He was well-built and his hands were rough. A man used to working hard, she noted with approval. He was tall for a fae, too, probably five-foot-six, and he had close-cropped brown hair. Practical.

She said, "So, your mother and my father were siblings-of-half, through our grandfather."

"Yes, I've heard our parents were very close a couple centuries ago, but life took them in different directions—your father to farming crops on the other side of the Veil, my mother as a... servant... of the elves. I'm happy to find I have a cousin who is still alive. Not all my cousins have been so lucky. So, how can I help my new friend today?"

Bells fought the urge to frown. Fae of blood simply did not rush through meeting for the first time. It wasn't the done thing. Very well, she'd get right to the point. "I'm here at my father's request to buy metal, which I've already arranged downstairs with your clerks..."

"...But?"

"But, I'm also looking for the numbers and street names—"

"The address."

"Okay, the address, for a dragon I once met, Jaekob, son of the dragons' First Councilor. I know he's here but didn't realize the city would be so large." Hawking's mouth ticked upward at one corner, amused for some reason. After a moment of silence, she continued, "I'd consider it a Favor Given, from my family to you."

She felt a thrill of triumph as he lost his smirk. She'd made it an official debt rather than just a courtesy between blood family. Hopefully, his merchant instincts would give that value where blood relation hadn't.

The silence stretched on awkwardly, his gaze never wavering. Then, he nodded. "Very well. You're blood, so I'll give you the address and keep this between us, and as my way of apologizing for my rudeness—I really am too busy for this, I wasn't lying—I'll have my clerks give you anything you need to resupply you for your trip home, free of charge. I have a wagon headed out beyond your village, leaving tomorrow, so if you're here in the morning, I can have them give you a ride home."

"That's beyond generous, cousin. I thank you."

"Just one more thing, though. Why do you want to see the First Councilor's heir?" He said it casually, but something made the hair on her arms stand up.

She kept her face a mask of stone, trying to hide her sudden caution. "As I said, I met him once. He invited me to say hello. I doubt I'll ever be back in this city, so I wanted to take advantage of the invitation."

There. That should be innocent enough, and if he was reading her aura, he wouldn't see a lie. She couldn't put her finger on just why she thought it mattered, though.

Hawking smiled and this time, it reached his eyes. They sparkled merrily as he grinned. "Okay. That's quite a tale. If you come back someday, you simply must tell me the whole story. But regardless, if you wait downstairs, I'll have someone look up the address and what time your 'friend' Jaekob should be home. A word of warning, though—get there at the right time. Too early and you'll stand out, and I can't guarantee your safety. Not even shadow-walking will hide you very long. And if you get there too late, the First Councilor will be home again, settled in inside, and they see no one after hours. So, timing is key. Is that help enough?"

Bells nodded, grinning. "Yes, of course. I can't tell you how much I appreciate it." His smile was infectious and it put her arm hair at ease, too. "I'll wait downstairs. Thanks again. If you get out our way, you must visit. After all, we owe you a debt."

They said their goodbyes, touching foreheads, and then she made her way downstairs. She felt good about her chances for the first time since she'd first thought of finding Jaekob again. She was light as a feather as she resupplied her pack and confirmed her order would be filled in the morning. When the clerk slipped a piece of paper into her hand, along with her receipt, her heart practically burst.

Tomorrow morning... She hadn't thought it would be so soon, and it meant she could head home right away. That was vital for her father to have any chance at finishing the troll's mace.

She made her way outside as quickly as she could and managed to hold her excitement long enough to get back into the market crowd. Then, she skipped for joy as she set out across the market. Time to find a place to hole up until it was closer to the time written on her note.

It had turned out to be a good day, after all.

As the dawning light streamed through the window into the abandoned human house, waking her gently, Bells stretched and smiled. She couldn't wait to see Jaekob again. He was going to make the world right again, he just had to, and this time, she wasn't going to take no for an answer.

She flicked her hand and the faint shadow which covered her and all her possessions faded away. It was a weak spell that wouldn't have stopped a Pure actively searching for someone in the room, nor fooled the senses of a were paying attention, but it was enough to make a casual observer's eyes glide over her, unseeing. A useful spell for any fae while traveling.

Once she'd risen and snacked on some of her dried foods, she finished dressing and headed out. She had chosen a spot only two blocks from Jaekob's house, and finding shadows would be fairly easy because of the low morning sun.

Once she spotted the house, though, she froze. It was no house—it was a mansion. It could have held all the people in her village comfortably. Heck, probably their houses, too. Status clearly came with privileges... Maybe she was wrong to come here. Anyone who lived in a house so obscenely rich wouldn't care about their own people, much less the disposable fae. What if they detained her for daring to try to talk to her betters?

A dozen such thoughts flew through her mind, doubt eating away at her resolve.

No! She shook her head to clear them away and placed her hand on a patch of grass to draw comfort and positive energy from the growing things and the crawling things beneath them. The doubt lifted. So, what if any of that happened? She and her family would be dead in a few days, anyway, if she didn't at least try. And she couldn't imagine dragons doing anything worse to her than the troll would do when he returned to collect his mace. He was probably going to do it even if she did get back in time for Father to forge it. With her resolve strengthened, she waited for the time she'd been given. It was only ten minutes away.

She passed the time by weaving a sight spell, idly curious about the protections the property had. Impressive... there was a full dome over the property, a protective spell that would block any magic she was strong enough to cast. It looked powerful enough to stop a hundred fae spells. Interwoven with the ice-blue protective energy, a mesh of red threads ran throughout the dome. Ah, so even physical access was blocked. It meant that they'd have to lower their dome to leave or return, she realized, but it was also much stronger than a selective spell, one that would allow some to pass and still block others. All-or-nothing was always stronger.

She wondered what else in life that could apply to.

The dome would vanish when someone left, and that would be her opportunity. Clever of Hawking to know all that. She'd have to swing back by and thank him later, assuming Jaekob didn't just melt her with dragonfire when he saw her, of course.

One minute before the listed time of 6:45 AM, Bells let her shadow-walk fade away and crossed the street, her heart in her throat and her stomach churning.

The front door opened, and a powerfully-built man walked out wearing a human business suit. Even from a distance, she could see the suit was of the finest quality. He was walking down the empty driveway toward the street, but just as he reached it, he seemed to notice her. His head whipped toward her and he paused for a second before walking the rest of the way down to meet her.

Her stomach flip-flopped, threatening to unload itself, and she swallowed hard. When he came within a few feet of her, she blurted, "I'm so sorry I couldn't come up to meet you, I would have, but there was a shell, and—"

"Whoa," he said. "Do I know you? I have to be at a meeting in ten minutes, but you can make an appointment with my secretary."

No, no, no. He was supposed to smile and be happy to see her... "Jaekob, don't you recognize me?"

Or maybe, she realized after she'd spoken, the shell might have blocked her scent. He had said that was how he would know her, after all.

The man grinned widely and seemed to relax. "You're mistaken. I'm Mikah, Jaekob's father. You must have met him in his dragon form, I take it. Is he expecting you?"

Even being friendly as he was, his aura of authority and power was intimidating and she had to fight the urge to crawl away under a rock somewhere. She was stupid for thinking a dragon would talk to a fae. Except that Jaekob actually had talked to her. Well, there was no point running away now. "Yes, when the dragons were finally Rising into the world, I met Jaekob. He made it clear he would recognize me when we met again."

There. That wasn't a lie. If he was looking for a dishonest aura, he wouldn't find one on her, and she would have been stunned if he weren't checking it.

He cocked his head but kept a faint smile on his face. So, at least she wasn't going to get burned to ashes today. Not yet.

"Very well," he said. "I'm about to leave, but you can come in and go to the door. Security will check you through. I don't think he has anything major planned today. Do behave, though, fae. Ta-ta." He waved his hands in an intricate pattern, and as the shell vanished, the air rushed into the suddenly-empty space it had left behind.

From the corner of her eye, Bells caught movement. She'd had her senses extended as far as a mere fae like her could send them because she was scared of being caught out in the open by a troll or something. Her senses told her there were four—no, five—people moving in quickly from the shadows across the street. Two trolls, two weres, and an elf.

"Sir!" she cried. Mikah had one leg raised into the air and the beginnings of wings were sprouting from his back as he summoned his dragon form to take off.

Catching the tone in her voice, he stopped mid-transformation and looked at her, his expression confused. "What is—"

Before he finished his sentence, she felt a flare of energy coming from the weres, and a different sort of energy flare from the elf. The weres had transformed into their most fearsome forms, she assumed, as her senses told her they were rushing across the street at impossible speeds. The elf, however, sent a bolt of energy streaking toward Mikah.

And he hadn't seen it.

Bells flung up her arm, hand outstretched toward Mikah, snap-firing her fae version of a shield. It was really more like a thick wall of heavy resistance. She saw the energy bolt hit her shield, and it slowed enough to see it passing through as her barrier disintegrated.

But it was enough. The split-second gave Mikah time to duck, and the bolt passed harmlessly over his head. He shouted one word, and she felt the power of the dome shield return. She spun to face the danger, realizing she'd just put herself between an enemy she couldn't hope to fight and their target she couldn't reach. By Creation, she was done for.

A bolt streaked toward her, but just before it struck her in her face, it seemed to hit something and splashed outward, like a melon thrown against a wall, before it faded away.

Whoa. She was inside the wall, she realized. Mikah had thrown the shell back up knowing she was far enough in to be protected. She spun to face him. "What if I were an assassin?" she cried, feeling a weird mix of anger and concern.

Mikah closed his eyes and muttered under his breath for a moment, then turned to her and smiled. "You saved me much trouble, youngling. That bolt would have frozen me mid-transformation, just long enough for those two weres you see running away to reach me at my most vulnerable."

"I did?" Had she? Huh. Yeah, it seemed she had.

The dragon laughed out loud. "Yes, fae. I may have defeated them anyway—but I may not have."

Just as he finished his sentence, she saw a dozen bursts of flame above them, all up and down the street, from a wing of dragons diving and flaming. Where their dragonfire struck a building, it seemed to explode from the impact, sending burning debris in all directions.

"Well," Mikah said when she didn't respond, "I guess I'm missing my meeting. Let's get you inside and take care of that wound."

Wound? What wound? She found herself frantically trying to see every part of herself as if he'd said a Ramarispider from beyond the Veil was on her. Right away, she found it—a big chunk of her side had been vaporized, just over her hip. The half-circle of missing flesh was the size of a large apple. It looked mostly cauterized, and wisps of smoke still rose from the burned flesh.

The world tilted crazily as she stared at Mikah's silently moving mouth, and the ground rushed up to slam into her. As her vision faded around the edges, another face came into view. Just before all turned black, her last thought was that the new, younger man was almost angelic. What an odd thought. She somehow knew without a doubt that it had been Jaekob, come to help her, after all.

The first thing Bells became aware of was a terrible, searing pain in her side. The second thing was a hushed conversation from nearby.

"She'll be up soon, but I'm already late for a meeting I cannot miss." It was a gruff male voice she didn't recognize.

"It's fine, Father. I'll be here. I'm not going anywhere until my shoulder heals up, which will take a few hours, but I should be good by tonight for the gala."

"I wish you hadn't confirmed her story about knowing you. She's not our responsibility, but we had to bring her in and treat her once you acknowledged having known her."

"Yeah, well, she might have saved your life, Fa. Maybe some gratitude."

The older voice—Mikah's, she realized—grunted. "All right. You have a point. Just don't let her steal anything. You know how fae have light fingers."

Bells was fighting the urge to sit up and defend herself from the accusation when she heard the sound of a door opening and closing, followed by silence. She struggled to lift her head but couldn't. She tried to call out, but her desert-dry throat was choked and it took too much effort.

The blackness closed over her again.

Her eyes flicked open, but the bright light hurt them and she squeezed them shut again. She tried to remember where she was, but her side was on fire and she couldn't concentrate.

A man's voice said, "Welcome back to the world, little fae."

Jaekob? She cracked one eye open and saw a dragon in his human form sitting in a plush office chair beside her... bed? She was in a bed. Memories trickled back, but not fast enough.

"Thank you. What happened?" Her throat was still painfully dry, and her voice cracked on the last word.

"Here, take a sip of this. Just a sip, mind you." Jaekob propped her head up with one hand and with the other, helped her drink from a small plastic cup. It felt like rain in a desert in her throat, a welcome relief. "Now that you're awake, I want to thank you for risking yourself to help the First Councilor. Um, my father. Obviously, we can't just have you leave here in your condition, especially not with whoever attacked us no doubt looking for you."

"Thanks?" She wasn't sure where the conversation was headed, but his tone bothered her. She didn't think he sounded very welcoming. She asked again, "What happened?"

"Well. That's open to interpretation. There are dragon guards outside the door, by the way, so please don't try to leave. Not until we get to the bottom of this."

"Okay... but will you just answer my question, at least? The last thing I remember, I had just realized I was hurt. It looked bad." She reached her hand out to move the sheet covering her so she could look at the wound, but something stopped her. Restraints?

Jaekob smiled wanly as she pulled against glyph-charmed leather straps. He looked angelic, like he should be shining. Chiseled features, high cheekbones above a firm, angular jaw... She blinked as she realized she was staring.

He said, "Sorry about having to bind you, but our security chief insisted, at least until we know more. Tell me, why were you there? And why at that exact time?"

A chill ran down her spine. "But, I saved him," she blurted. "How could you think I had something to do with the attack?"

Jaekob let out a deep breath. "I don't think that. But then again, I could be wrong. You wouldn't be the first person to try to take Mikah out. Nor to try killing me, for that matter. If you were a part of it, well, it almost worked."

Despite her precarious position, her irritation rose. She didn't have much, but she had her integrity and she wasn't going to let them take that from her so easily. "Like I said, I tried to save him. Does that sound like I was working with whoever attacked him?"

"Nope. That's why you're here instead of doing what the security chief wanted. Trust me, dying would have been better than the questioning he'd have put you through."

Bells shifted on the bed, trying to alleviate the pain a bit, and a fiery bolt of agony shot through her, making her groan out loud. Through clenched teeth, she asked, "Am I dying?"

His winsome grin reappeared. "Hardly. What would people whisper about us if we let the First Councilor's rescuer die when we had the chance to save her? No, you're healing fast. One of our most trusted elven healers laid hands on you, and his spell is working on your wound even now." His smile faded as he added, "It'll take time, though."

"Thank you. I'm just a fae. Such a service must have cost dearly." She watched intently for his reaction.

Jaekob's expression gave nothing away, however, and he waved her off with one hand. "You don't have to worry about the cost," he said, and his mouth twitched upward at her relieved expression. "But I do need to ask why you're here, and why you showed up when you did. Be honest—Bells, right?— because I'll know if you lie to me."

She pursed her lips but quickly forced her expression back to neutral. The last thing she needed was to offend the second most important person this side of the Veil, not after he said he believed her. "I came to see you, of course, but you figured that out, I'm sure. My cousin gave me your address and told me to be here right at a quarter to seven. He said that was the only time I could see you."

Jaekob's eyes narrowed.

She cocked her head, confused. "My cousin is a kind, generous man. I'm sure he's not involved."

His reply came almost instantly. "You're a fae from a village miles from here, and Hawking has been here since the Pures took this city, since before the Dragons' Rising."

How did he know her cousin's name? They must have checked her out somehow and found him that way. Family trees were kept by the elves, and they did a thorough job of it for less than charitable reasons. But that meant she'd been unconscious longer than she thought. "We have the same grandfather, but not the same grandmother. I had never met him, but blood is blood. We help our own; it's the fae way. He gave me a good deal on the metal I need to save my family, and found out your address for me—"

"Wait." He leaned forward, and she could practically smell the suspicion emanating from him. "Your family is in danger and he helped you, in exchange for coming here at one exact time. I'm sorry, but that doesn't paint you out to be an innocent bystander. It sounds like his fee wasn't in trade goods, but in a favor."

Bells felt her face twist, reflecting the indignation she felt. "Blood helps blood, and that's why he helped me. He didn't say I had to come, either. That was my idea, and half the reason I came to this city at all."

"Okay, okay," Jaekob said, holding up both hands toward her. "Relax. I see in your eyes you aren't lying, and I trust my instincts. But you have to admit, it looks suspicious. And I'm sorry about your cousin."

"Why sorry?" A knot formed in her stomach. *Please don't let it mean what I think it means.*

"He was taken in by dragon security forces for questioning. The sort of questioning I'm glad you were spared. And before you ask, there's nothing I can do for him, nor would I even if I could. You don't know him at all, and there's—well, there's more going on in this city than you know."

She nodded, fighting back tears. She'd brought that on her cousin, to her shame.

Jaekob said, "Now, please. I've asked several times, and I want a straight answer this time. Why are you here to see me?"

Sort of like she'd asked him three times before getting a straight answer. She frowned. Still blinking back tears, she said, "There's... There is a troll who says my father owes him a mace. I didn't know about those work orders. The troll will be back in a few days, and if we don't have his mace ready for him to take to the Inscribers, it will be the death of my family. And of me."

"I see," he said, and he wrinkled his nose like he could smell a troll at that moment.

She felt her anger rising as she spoke, a dam cracking under the pressure from everything that she'd seen and done the last few days and years of virtual enslavement. It made her reckless. "I remember you when you first Rose, only ten years ago—a blink, even for fae—and you were howling for blood and justice. But you haven't done anything since then, not that I can see. My village is still half-starved, and the elves and other Pures still use us almost like slaves. Where is *my* justice?"

She knew it was foolish to speak to any Pure that way, much less the dragon heir himself, but she couldn't stop the words from coming.

Jaekob didn't seem offended, though. He sat quietly and listened until she was done. Then, he reached his hand out and put it on hers. "I sympathize, but I'm not the one to help you. It's wrong, what is happening to your family, but—"

"But what?" Bells cut him off, her voice steely. "You can't just sit by while the Pures rule this world into dust like the humans did. How is this any better? The elves tore the Veil to come save the Earth, but—"

"Stop," Jaekob said, and though he hadn't raised his voice, something about his tone froze her in fear. He clenched his jaw, taking a deep breath through his nose. "My father is trying to create a new peace. He wants to end the war against humans and the war between the White King and the Black Court. He thinks we can be better than humans and live in peace."

"You don't think so." Bells said it as a statement rather than a question. It was obvious how he felt about it.

"The world doesn't deserve peace. The Pures die in droves fighting each other, humans are near extinction, and you fae are slaves. That's the world the Pure Council created."

"It's not the world we deserve, Jaekob. The fae don't have a choice in all this. We're victims, and you can stop it."

"Maybe, maybe not. But I'm not going to try. You say the fae have no choice, but that's not true. You could refuse. If you all refused to work, what could the other Pures do about it? Kill you all? Hardly."

"You think we should all just commit suicide? You're wrong about what they'd do to us. All we want is to be left alone with our plants and forests. Thanks to the weres, we can't even commune with the forests anymore, not this time around."

"Yes. Dying for your cause is a choice you *could* make, but you don't. This world and everyone in it... I think this world is getting exactly what it created.

None of it deserves the peace my father is trying to create. It deserves what it's getting."

"Even my family? Is that what you're saying? We deserve to be some troll's dinner over a lie he told?"

Jaekob's steady gaze and iron silence answered her question well enough.

She asked, "So why did you all Rise if dragons aren't going to do anything for anyone but yourselves?"

She hoped her tone made it clear she was questioning him as a person, too. All the dragons. She'd likely be flamed for questioning him. It would be a faster, less painful death than what the troll would deliver, at least.

Jaekob shrugged instead of flaming her, though, and said, "The war made my kind Rise. It's always war when we awaken early. This war, however, exists because the Council is divided. The last time we awoke was a blink of an eye ago, maybe fifty or sixty years, when the human world was divided and killing itself yet again."

"And you did something about it. Unlike now."

"We helped the side of right to win that war against the Germans—again—but what did humans do with the opportunity they were given? They declared war on the Earth herself. They fought a hundred smaller wars instead of one big one. They mastered propaganda and the few dominated the many by turning everyone against each other. And frankly, that's no different than what the Pures are doing. I'll have no part of it. The world can tear itself apart just fine without my help."

Bells sat dumbfounded. "Wait... Dragons Rise to fight for justice, and you were awoken this time by an unjust war, like every time. But because the oppressors are Pures, *now* you think the victims earned it? There's a word for that sort of attitude."

"Logical?"

"Hypocritical."

Jaekob's eyes narrowed and Bells thought she saw a wisp of smoke rise from his nostrils. Oh Creation, she'd finally pushed her luck too far with this Pure. She braced herself but met his gaze.

He didn't move his hand from hers, however, and the expression passed quickly. He looked away as he said, "You're free to stay here until you're healed. But you do not belong here, and as soon as you're able, I'm driving you back to your village. Your fate there is your problem, little fae. And I just hope that my father figures out his peace crusade is pointless. Then we can go back to slumber for another century or two."

She opened her mouth to reply but he stood abruptly and walked out, leaving her to dwell on too many things. Like, why wouldn't he just fly her home? Or was carrying a fae beneath his pride? If so, why drive her back at all? The many questions swirling together were overwhelming, and her wounds had her weak and tired. Mind spinning pointlessly in a dozen directions, she fell into a restless sleep.

Two days later, Bells felt healed enough to get out of bed for more than a minute or two. It had been a long, tedious two days, although being served by dragons was a story she'd be telling her grandkids... Oh wait, she was going to be devoured by a troll long before then. She pushed that thought aside, though. She wasn't dead yet, and it wasn't wrong to enjoy the irony of being served by the purest of the Pures.

She swung her feet off the bed and stretched to one side, feeling the freshly-knit wound on her side as it pulled against her movement. It was incredible what power the elf healer had used to save her life.

Even if she had survived on her own, without that magic her recovery would have taken months and she'd probably have been disabled for the rest of her life. When the healer had come in only an hour earlier to remove his healing spell and the charcoal-written glyph on her waist, he had said she would fully heal in just a few more days. Muscle and skin knitting together would be the last of her recovery. Her insides were already healed up nicely.

She looked down at the sheepskin slippers on the floor awaiting her feet and smiled at the thought of Mikah's kindness. Being given a get-well gift by the most powerful man in this or any other world was quite a story to tell when she got home.

Unfortunately, Mikah had only come in the one time, and she suspected that was only because she'd saved him from being injured or killed by assassins. He gave her about five minutes of his time, but judging by the dark circles under his eyes and his sunken cheeks, those five minutes were probably dearly bought. He had seemed kind, however. Kind, but hard. All dragons were—they were warriors to their core, protectors by nature.

Well, today she was going home. She let out a sigh. Her father would only have three days to forge the mace, which probably wasn't enough time. Not to craft with the fae quality the troll would demand. And the whole family would probably go without sleep all three days, taking up Father's responsibilities around the farm in the hopes he would complete it in time to save them all. Three exhausting days, at the end of which she and her family were probably dead.

At least she'd had these two days in the dragons' mansion. It was an experience enjoyed by no other fae she'd ever heard of. All told, she decided, hers had been a life of adventure by anyone's standards, especially the fae. A life well lived.

Slippers on her feet, she pulled on a plush cotton robe they let her use and limped to the door, her side aching like dull fire with every step. She hoped that would heal better by the time she had to pick up some of her father's chores and resume her own.

She made her way to the kitchen. Her room was quite near there, probably meant for the cooking servants. No doubt the room's usual occupant had no problem being forced to stay in another of the mansion's better rooms during her stay.

She turned the corner and saw their kitchen for the first time. It was larger than her family's hut and full of the humans' cooking gizmos. The kitchen could have served an entire tavern, she decided. Or one of the human restaurants, even.

An almost elderly-looking man wearing all white pants and some sort of white coat stood at one counter, hand-mixing something in a big metal bowl. "Good morning, sir."

He looked over and smiled wanly. "Good morning, miss. Would you like me to make you something to eat? You look like you could use it."

Bells grinned. She was hungry, but in truth, she just couldn't get over being spoken to kindly by Pures. "Please, I'd love something. Whatever is convenient, though—please don't go out of your way for the likes of me."

He cocked his head and raised one eyebrow. "The likes of you? Young lady, all I see is a lovely young woman with the courage to save a dragon's life."

"You know who I am?" she asked, surprised and blinking.

"Of course. You don't really think there are any secrets when the household staff knows about it, do you? We gossip worse than elves when we're by ourselves. Just call me Chef." His face lit into a grin, his eyes twinkling.

Bells couldn't help but grin back. "I'm not used to being a center of attention, Chef."

"I'm sure you aren't," he said, his smile fading. "But you can't imagine the chaos that would come if they'd killed Mikah. The shadow war would have turned into a real one and the streets would run with blood. If an old man could give you some advice?"

She nodded, curious about this "shadow war" he'd mentioned.

"The lowly are just as noble as the high-born. Often, more so. What you did took courage and no one can take that away from you, whatever your station in life."

She didn't know how to respond. Getting such praise from a dragon—a dragon!—was intimidating. She looked away and grabbed her elbows. "Thanks."

Chef chuckled and started moving around the kitchen, grabbing ingredients from the massive refrigerator and some cabinets. "How do strawberries-and-cream waffles sound? No, no, it's not a bother," he said when she started to object. "You've earned a nice meal before you're kicked back out into the real world."

She climbed up onto one of the barstools at the kitchen island's far side and rested her elbows on the countertop. "Do you like working here?" she asked, mostly because she couldn't think of anything else to say.

"I do indeed," Chef replied as he cracked eggs into a bowl then grabbed a bag of flour. "Mikah is one of the best people I've had the privilege of serving. His vision would make the world a great place for all if only people weren't so short-sighted and greedy. Pures and humans alike, in this old man's opinion."

That was practically heresy. Her jaw dropped.

He continued, "Let them punish me. I'm old. I've watched human empires rise and fall, young lady, and I've seen whole new continents discovered and then exploited. In all those years, I haven't noticed much difference between the Pures and the human animals. But they're just animals, following their instincts. We Pures are supposed to be elevated, with higher, nobler minds. I don't see much evidence for that belief, though."

Okay, that really was heresy. She glanced around nervously but saw no one else nearby. She recalled what Jaekob had said about humans—they were Pures, too, who had simply lost their connection to the Great Creation. "If Pures are no different than humans, then why do we have our powers and they don't?"

Chef clicked the stove on and set a frying pan on the burner. "Assuming they ever were Pures—and that's just an old fairy tale as far as I know—I couldn't tell you why they became un-Pure. I wouldn't be surprised if we all do eventually. Perhaps it's just because their generations pass by in the blink of an eye, so their sins compounded faster. Who knows?"

They sat in a comfortable silence for a while as he finished cooking her pancakes, and when he set them in front of her, beautifully plated, her stomach growled loud enough for Chef to hear it and chuckle. While she ate, he went about cleaning up and working some more on whatever he'd been doing when she came in. It looked like some sort of pastry with bacon, little bite-sized morsels. She wouldn't have minded being here when those were finished.

She ate all but a few bites of the massive pancake pile he'd given her, slid the plate away, and grinned. "Thank you so very much. When I die, I'm going to think back on this meal as my happy place."

"Well, I doubt you'll remember it in five hundred years, but thanks."

"No," she replied, smiling wistfully at him. "More like three days. But truly, thank you for the fantastic food and for treating me so well. I'm not used to that from the other Pures."

"Three days? I'm so sorry. That seems a terrible fate for the one who saved the First Councilor's life. May I ask how you are to die?" he asked as casually as one might ask what was for dinner.

"A troll says my family owes him a war mace but I never got that command. I came to the city for metal so we might try to make it in time. He's going to eat my family if we fail, but he probably will anyway. You know trolls."

"I do know them, yes. Some are good enough, but they don't have any inborn sense of empathy for others. I'm sorry. Perhaps the heir, Jaekob, might give you one of the armory's maces to spare your family?"

"He hasn't offered."

Chef frowned but nodded. "Yes, he's been rather defeatist lately. Melancholy, even. I think he feels the world these days deserves what it gets."

Bells shrugged. Jaekob had told her as much, but if he hadn't shared that with his family chef, it wasn't her place to tell him. "Thank you again for the meal, Chef. And for the conversation. I wish I had more time to talk to you. Jaekob is driving me home in a little bit, but I will remember you."

Chef wiped his hands on a small towel, which he hung back up on the stove handle when he was done. "I'll remember you too, young Miss Bells. If I could help, I would, but I wish you luck and joy. Just remember one thing, though."

"What's that?" She hopped off the stool and stopped at the counter's edge, waiting for his reply before she left.

"When you see a person who is jaded and sour, it's not because they're dark of heart. It's because they had high ideals that were crushed by life's experiences. Do not judge master Jaekob too harshly, though I know that must be hard given what you are facing."

"Thanks." Bells gave him her best curtsy, a sign of respect, and he smiled and waved before she left.

As she made her way back to her room to get dressed, Chef's last words echoed in her mind. She wished the old dragon was right, but in her experience, the jaded people in this world simply didn't care much about others.

When Bells saw the car awaiting them, her eyes went wide and a grin spread from ear to ear, but then pursed lips replaced the smile. She reached up to rub her ear as her eyes darted everywhere but at Jaekob. "Is... Can we do this? I mean, is it dangerous?"

Jaekob chuckled. "It's perfectly safe. And far more comfortable than a carriage or wagon. How long did you have to walk to get here?"

"Oh, hours and hours. But how does it run? The humans' fuel has all gone bad long ago." She wanted to leap into the wondrous machine but, at the same time, to run as far away from it as possible.

"Pixies, of course. We hire them to power the machines when we need them. They're part of my staff, so it doesn't actually cost us anything more to use their services." He put his hand on her back and gently coaxed her toward the car.

The thing was huge, and human lettering proclaimed it to be a "Cadillac." It had an odd, glittery black paint job and four doors. In front of it were two of the human-built two-wheeled cars. Motorcycles? Yeah, that was it. And two more idled behind the car. The riders she recognized as Dragon Guardians, Jaekob's bodyguards.

Bells let Jaekob guide her to the car's rear door, which he opened for her and said, "If you please, you'll ride in back with me instead of in front so we can chat while we drive. It shouldn't take long. These cars go faster than horses can and never tire out."

She got in a bit awkwardly but managed to slide to the far side. Thankfully, the seats were leather and not one of the toxic manufactured fibers the humans loved so much. All in all, the seat was amazingly comfortable, though she wondered how it would feel if she were stuck inside for a few hours on a long trip.

"Thanks," she said as he got in and closed the door behind him. She was briefly interrupted when two more people got into the front seats and slammed their doors shut. Then she continued, "I've never been in one of these. I was born right after the last big human war, the second German one, but my family are farmers."

Jaekob nodded. Of course farmers didn't need cars. They needed to stay put and farm, not move around. It was their lot in life.

Five miles passed with blinding speed. In mere minutes, they were already outside the city.

Amazing. "And you said it can go this speed for as long as you want it to?"

Jaekob, looking out the side window, nodded. "Until we change out the faerie powering the engine. It's tiring for them so they prefer not to do it for more than a couple hours at a time. Half the container space in back is storage—where your backpack is—and the other half we converted into a nice space for the fairies who are off duty. Twenty of 'em for this trip, just in case we need to drive farther than expected."

Bells nodded but worried for them. Sure, fairies were only two inches tall, but Jaekob made it sound like they had a choice in the matter. Fae had no choice. Even those little tricksters were treated better than her kind... Or maybe it was just that Jaekob was a nicer master than the elf who controlled her village. She wasn't about to ask, though.

When she felt the car slowing, she turned to Jaekob and bit her lower lip nervously.

"Don't worry," he said, smiling faintly, "there's just a jam up ahead. Want to stretch your legs and take a look? Maybe you can help."

They'd only been in the car for a few minutes, but if Jaekob needed her to give him an excuse to go check out the cluster of people ahead blocking the road, she didn't mind. "Sure. I'm happy to help. They're fae."

When they climbed out through Jaekob's door, though, she saw there weren't only fae. Two wagons had scraped each other in passing, it looked like, as one had both wheels sheared off. It lay on its side and its full load of vegetables was scattered in the mud. Other fae had stopped to help, but a troll was there, also, barking orders at the fae. Six of them struggled to lift the wagon so they could clear the road, something the troll could have done with one hand. The six weren't having any success, though, despite trying hard enough to make their faces beet-red with effort.

Jaekob called out, "Troll. We're trying to get by. Do you know how long this will take?"

Bells glanced at him and saw he was smiling, and his tone had been friendly, not demanding.

The troll turned and his eyes grew wide. "My prince!" he said, surprised. Jaekob's expression turned irritated. "We'll clear this right away, sir."

Jaekob looked down at her and said, "It doesn't look like you'll need to dirty yourself. If the fae can't move it and the troll won't do it, my Guardians and I will help—"

He stopped suddenly and his eyes narrowed. Bells turned back just in time to see the troll stomp to the wagon and knock two fae backhanded across the road. He grabbed the wagon's underside with both hands and flung it at least ten feet. It landed with a *crack* and split in half, bits flying off in a cloud of dirt.

Bells let out a squeak and covered her mouth with both hands, eyes wide.

"What is it?" Jaekob looked back at the scene, head tilted, then back at her and said, "Well, next time they'll have to take better care of their wagon. Too bad about the load but at least it was just vegetables."

"You don't understand..."

"They'll just grow more," he replied, rolling his eyes. "It's what farmers do."

"No, they'll never get the chance to. When they get back to their village, their elf is going to let his trolls eat them as a warning to the rest. Even if he doesn't, the next load is going to come out of their personal allotment. They're going to starve to death and *then* get eaten, or they'll get killed the minute they get home empty-handed."

Jaekob stumbled back a step, mouth falling open.

Bells blurted out before she could stop the words, "Don't pretend you didn't know they'll die over this." She hissed his own words back at him, "That's just what farmers do."

He shook his head faintly. "No, I didn't. I mean, I know fae are mostly farmers—your magic makes you the best choice for that—but that's the natural order of things. Being killed over a wagon of turnips or whatever, that's...barbaric."

"That's elves, *Master* Jaekob."

His eyes narrowed for just a moment, but to her surprise, she found she didn't much care what he did to her. If he killed her for insolence, he'd probably do it quick and painless, unlike what awaited her family in a few days.

"Get in the car," he said quietly, and she couldn't tell if he was angry or not. His face was a mask, rigidly neutral.

She didn't make him ask twice, sliding wordlessly into the back seat.

The next twenty minutes passed in silence, Jaekob gazing out his window with a faraway look, leaving her to her own dark thoughts.

As she watched the scenery pass by, she recognized the outskirts of her village and sat up straighter, trying to get a better look ahead of them through the side window.

Jaekob said, "Driver, stop." He turned to Bells, and at her confused expression, said, "Why don't we walk in together? I need to talk to the foreman anyway. Just business."

She nodded. So that was the real reason he wanted to drive her out there. At least this dragon was efficient. She followed him out of the car, and though she'd hoped to see the faerie "break room" in the cargo area, one of his Guardians had already retrieved her backpack. She had forgotten that dragons could talk mind-to-mind with each other. She smiled her thanks and took the pack, slinging it over her shoulders. "Okay, if you're ready, I am honored to show you my humble village."

The Guardian smirked. "Humble is the word, all right."

Jaekob smiled but his tone was abrupt when he replied, "Be nice. We are in someone else's home, now." The Guardian bowed his head. Jaekob looked down at Bells. "Lead on, little fae."

Nervous, Bells straightened her clothes, ran her hands through her hair, and drew herself up. "Yes, sir," she said and started walking.

Immediately, every head in view turned toward her. Mouths dropped and within seconds, more people appeared, gawking.

Jaekob said softly, "Bells, why are they all dressed in rags? Yours aren't much better, but at least you're presentable. Are you among the wealthy in this village?"

Bells led him around a big mud puddle in the dirt trail that served as the village's main street. "We all wear rags. I'm wearing my older sister's nicest top, my mother's nicest skirt, and my brother's nicest jacket. As the youngest, my own clothes are hand-me-downs and even worse than most."

Jaekob followed in silence, his eyes scanning every detail in the village. His gaze lingered on a young girl who was missing one leg, and his eyes grew wide at the sight of a larger fae man pulling a small plow behind him, which was guided by his very young son.

When she got to her own hut, the door flew open and her mother wrapped her in a big embrace. Her father was next, gathering them both in his arms. After a second, though, he left his wife and daughter hugging and turned to Jaekob. His jaw dropped and he instantly bowed low, touching his forehead to the ground.

"Rise," Jaekob said, softly enough that Bells barely heard him, but her father scrambled to his feet. Then Jaekob pushed his way into the hut, not forcefully but moving inexorably like an iceberg. Bells and her family got out of his way.

"I am Jaekob," he said in introduction. "Your daughter was gravely injured saving my father, the First Councilor, from an assassination attempt. No—no—she's fine. My doctors healed her and I drove her home by way of thanks." He looked around the hut, his gaze pausing on every crack in the wall, every missing floorboard, every empty candle sconce. "You have a lovely home."

How polite. Bells fought back a scowl and a grin at the same time. "I got the metal, Father," she said, handing him her backpack.

"Thank you, but we can talk about that when we don't have company. Don't be rude," he said, smiling. To Jaekob, he bowed slightly and said, "Thank you for driving her home. You've saved her a day of travel. That's more helpful than you know."

The dragon nodded. "Yes, she's told me of your dilemma. She negotiated a good deal in the market, I believe. You should have enough to fend off that troll."

Father's eyes went wide. "She told you?"

Jaekob shrugged. "I asked. She had to. Tell me, why didn't you just advise your elf village leader about the troll? It is his or her job to fend off such predators. If the troll harms your family, that lowers the output, and he has to answer for that."

Bells shook her head and, with too loud a voice, said, "No. He delights in our suffering, and he'll make up the production by forcing the surviving villagers to work harder. Everyone will be terrified after watching their friends and neighbors—my family—being eaten in the middle of the street."

"You won't run? I would." He raised one eyebrow at her.

"Of course we can't run. Where could a fae go? We're bound to our village by the Pures, just slaves. If we showed up in another village, we'd be turned in. If we hid in the wilderness, we'd be hunted by weres for sport. There is nowhere to go."

He changed the subject, asking Mother about the family and many of the knickknacks her family had accumulated. Well, the Dragon Prince had impeccable manners, at least in public, but Bells didn't miss the fact that his shoulders were slumped, arms crossed, and he wasn't meeting anyone's eyes when they talked. Was he affected by what he saw in the village? Surely he had known how things were, so close to his own home, right?

Or maybe not, since the Prince of Dragons was probably kept busy with his "regal duties." Or even shielded from the terrible things going on around him. She frowned at the thought. How could a ruler truly lead if he didn't know what was happening right under his nose—or snout, as the case may be?

After Jaekob said his polite goodbyes to Bells' family, his Guardians escorted him outside to the car. Bells politely accompanied him as well, intent on saying goodbye. Hopefully, the things he had seen would eat at him until he did something to help her family and her village, but if not, she actually found herself feeling better knowing that someone outside of her own kind would remember her and her family.

As they walked, she kept glancing at Jaekob. His shoulders were still slumped, his face troubled. She almost felt bad for the Dragon Prince. What he had seen obviously bothered him a great deal, which spoke well of him as a person as far as she was concerned. She also caught him glancing at her as they walked, but she didn't quite understand his expression when their eyes met, and he looked away each time she caught him looking.

When they got to the car, she said, "Thank you for bringing me home, and for saving my life in Philadelphia. Whatever happens to me and my family in a few days, I want you to know that I appreciate it and I think you're a good person. I hope that someday you'll be in a position to set things right so other fae don't suffer like my family."

He looked away again and took a deep breath, but didn't reply. He just stood there, looking tense and indecisive.

After several seconds of awkward silence, one of his Guardians said, "Sir, it's time to leave. Is there anything else that you need before we go?"

Jaekob held out a hand to her, fingers spread, and pursed his lips. He looked at Bells again and said, "Come with me." He glanced at his Guardians and added, "Stay here."

The Guardian shook his head curtly and said, "Sir, you know we can't do—"

"Silence," Jaekob snapped. "I am the First Councilor' heir and you will obey me." He clenched his jaw and stared at the Guardian until the man broke eye contact first and nodded.

"Yes, Prince."

The muscles in Jaekob's jaw and neck stood out. A vein throbbed faintly on his forehead. "Bells, would you be so kind as to escort me to your elf foreman?"

She didn't get the feeling it was a request. "Of course."

She walked with him toward the village center. When they were just out of earshot from the others, she begged, "Please don't do this. You're going to get my family killed even faster than the troll."

He pursed his lips, stopped, and gently—even tenderly—wiped the tears from her cheeks with his thumb, then cupped her face in his hands. They were strong hands, the rough hands of a warrior, yet his touch was so tender that he might have been holding a butterfly.

Heat rose in her cheeks and the corners of his lips turned up ever so slightly. He said, "Bells, I'm not going to get you in trouble. Trust me, please. Where is your foreman?"

At his touch, her throat closed up and she barely heard his words over the sound of her heart pounding in her ears. "I... he's—I think the pond he's at." No, stupid! Those weren't the right words. She felt suddenly too hot under her collar.

"Right. He's at the pond. I assume you mean his fish pond. Well, little fae, lead on." He smiled, and for the second time, she was struck by his easygoing, natural good looks. Rugged, not fancy, this prince. He probably looked even better dressed up, too. An image of him in his royal-red bandoleer down in the Warrens drifted through her mind.

She shook her head to clear those thoughts. What on Earth was wrong with her? "Yes, um. The fish pond." They stared at each other for about five heartbeats, then she spun on her heels and walked toward the nearby stream, feeling grateful he couldn't see her face. The breeze from walking felt good on her overheated neck.

A minute later, the stream appeared ahead. The foreman's fish pond was the largest and all the fae had to work together to take care of it. He sure wasn't going to lift a finger. Why work when he had captive fae? Arrogant son-of-a—

"Is that him?" Jaekob asked, pointing at a hooded figure near the pond holding a fishnet.

She nodded. "That's Nigel, yes."

What the heck was going on with her? When Jaekob stormed toward the man, who had his back to them, she froze for a moment, then scurried into a shadow and frantically started shadow-walking. Elves could detect a hidden fae, but not one using that ability—not unless they were looking right at her *and* trying to find her.

Jaekob said loudly, "Foreman Nigel. A word, please."

Nigel spun around, face already red with anger and mouth open to scream, until he realized who had dared to speak to him. At Bells' distance, all she could see for sure was that he stood ramrod-straight and bowed his head, but she couldn't hear their words. They spoke only for a minute, then Jaekob pointed toward the village's far end. The elf stormed off in that direction, fists clenched and leaning forward. Woe to the next fae he saw...

Jaekob watched him leave and then came back to where she hid, eyes searching the undergrowth. She let her shadow-walk fall away and he locked eyes with her. "There you are," he said, smiling. "You needn't worry about him anymore."

"What did you say? He's going to kill us before the troll does!" Bells' eyes flared wide and she grabbed her chest. Her knees almost buckled. "My family—"

"—will be fine," he interrupted. "I told him that whatever fate lay in store for you or any member of your family, that's what I would do to him. If you were devoured by a troll, he'd be breakfast for a dragon the very day, and if he raised your quotas, then he, too, would have a quota. One I'd make him work off personally."

"You didn't." She cocked her head. Why would a dragon do that for her? That was like a king mucking a stall for his stable hand. It just wasn't the done thing.

"I did. Your family should be safe now and that's the least I could do for the danger you put yourself in saving my father. Fa appreciates what you did, and so do I. But we're not done with that elf."

Bells felt herself grinning so big her cheeks hurt. This was no typical rich, snotty dragon. Naive, maybe, but a good man. "What else are you going to do to Nigel?"

"Not me. You. I'm going to take you back to Philadelphia to report him. No, no, don't worry—I'm going with you. They'll take *that* seriously, I guarantee it. The thing is, it's technically against the White King's commands for them to kill their fae, starve them, or even to treat them so horribly that they can't work anymore. Fae are Pures, not humans, and the elves' own beliefs mean they should treat you all better. But no one truly cares and no one does anything about it. I know that what you go through is so common as to be expected, right?"

"Yes," she said, her voice trailing away. "I didn't even know it wasn't official policy, or whatever you call it."

"The thing is, if the dragon heir goes with you while you file a complaint, they'll have to deal with it, and violating the White King's rules has only one penalty among the elves. Nor will you get into any trouble for moving around the city without a foreman's writ. Not while I'm with you."

"What's that?"

Jaekob grinned and shook his head. "Any fae in Philadelphia who isn't in the company of their Pure foreman or boss is in a heap of trouble if the guards check and feel mean that day. Normally they don't since they don't know whose master sent the fae and vendettas are common and nasty. But if you were to report an elf foreman without having such a writ, they might use it as an excuse to bury both the problem and you in one fell swoop."

That was the stupidest thing she'd ever heard. Well, almost. Could Jaekob be right? "But if you have to go to the administration center in order to report a foreman, how do they expect the fae to have written permission from that same foreman?"

Jaekob shrugged and lost his grin. "That's kind of the point. But you and I will sidestep that dilemma to report this disgusting elf, and I will make sure they handle it to the letter of their own law."

She rushed into him, wrapping her arms around him and burying her cheek in his chest for a second before stepping back. She was smiling and crying at the same time, and laughed awkwardly as she wiped her eyes. "Thank you. With your help, I can finally get justice. It won't change anything for the other fae, but you don't know how much it means to me that you're doing something, anything at all."

"I might know," he said cryptically, his face expressionless and his shoulders stiff. "Shall we go?"

She nodded and followed him to his waiting vehicle, feeling suddenly confused.

When they got to the city's outskirts, Jaekob's Guardians drew their motorcycles closer to the car and all heads turned to watch them go by. Only through force of will did Bells stop herself from trying to shadow-walk to hide from the danger she imagined everywhere around them. It might not have been her imagination, even, considering what had happened a few days earlier. But as they continued driving slowly through the city proper and no one launched a pixy missile at them, or whatever, she felt herself relaxing a bit. She kept alert but some of her tension faded.

Jaekob gently put his hand on her forearm. "You don't need to be afraid, little fae. Few would dare to try anything against me, especially not surrounded by Guardians. But just in case, this vehicle is also enchanted."

She fidgeted with her fingers but made herself smile and nod as the drive continued. After another ten minutes, she broke the silence. "Why is it taking so long to get there?" They were in a human vehicle, after all. They were a lot faster than horses.

"It's on the other end of town. We're going to the elves' regional HQ, after all. They don't care to mingle with the rest of us, so it's in the elf district."

"Oh." She watched a couple more blocks go by, but her thoughts drifted elsewhere and became troubled.

She must have let her thoughts show on her face, because he asked, "What's wrong, Bells?"

She took a deep breath and let it out slowly. "You know, what happened to my family was bad, and make no mistake, you're saving our lives. But how many others in just my little village are suffering under the elves just as I did? You're the Prince of Dragons. You could help so many more people if you wanted to, and I'm no more deserving than they are."

In her peripheral view, she saw him staring at her, but she didn't turn to look at him. He said, "That's not actually true, unfortunately. None of those fae helped my father. I don't owe them."

She furrowed her eyebrows, and this time, she did turn to look at him. "I'm not ungrateful, but you have to know that every fae in the region is living the same way I do. If you truly want to help me, you might try to make life a little more bearable for my people. They *all* need your help, and you can really make a difference in their lives. I just think it's a little... selfish. I don't mean to offend you, but that's the best word I could think of."

Jaekob's face flushed, and for a split second, she caught a sensation from his aura. He was powerful, physically and magically, and could squash her. But as quickly as she felt it, the sensation passed. "I'm sorry," he said. "I should control my temper better. I know you fae can feel auras."

"Survival thing."

"Sure. But I don't think it's fair to—oh, hold on..."

"What—"

Jaekob waved his hand, cutting her off. "Quiet."

She felt her own temper rising. She was about to say something—probably something stupid—when Jaekob's radio crackled.

"Sir, the Wards."

Jaekob didn't respond but sat frozen with his head cocked. Bells stared at him, watching his expression and feeling suddenly worried. She desperately wanted to ask questions but bit her lip to stay quiet. He had to concentrate, and she let him.

When he spoke again, he wasn't looking at her. He had a faraway look in his eyes, muttering, "Northwest section of the Dragon Quarter, by the elf border. Go!"

Jaekob pressed on the gas pedal. The car accelerated suddenly, pressing her back into her seat. The car, accompanied by the troop of motorcycles, sped dangerously, and she felt the tail end drifting as they took one corner after another at breakneck speeds. She gripped the leather seats tight enough to make her fingers turn white.

Jaekob's expression had become fierce. It kind of scared her until she reminded herself that he wasn't directing it at her personally. He said, "Before the Rising ten years ago, some elves found a way through our Wards down in Safeholme. They somehow got dragonblood and injected it into themselves. The Wards only allowed 'those with dragonblood in their veins' to pass, and so they got through, but not without triggering some alarms. Whoever just hit our Wards again is realizing we've had plenty of time to make changes over the last ten years."

She nodded. Through the windshield, she saw they were almost to the dockyards district. The whole place looked like bedlam, even from a distance, and there were Pures of various races fleeing past the car in the opposite direction. Most looked wounded. Without realizing it, Bells slipped into her shadow-walk, vanishing into the passenger seat floorboard. It was the only shadow available.

She felt the car accelerate even more as Jaekob jammed his foot onto the gas pedal.

As Jaekob drove closer to the docks, Bells curled up on the floorboards. The sounds outside the car grew louder and more frightening. She heard screams and even a couple of explosions. Her fae senses lit up as she felt battle magic being used throughout the district, growing stronger the farther she and Jaekob drove.

He looked down at her with his eyes glowing bright red. His gaze locked onto hers despite her actively shadow-walking. He said, "It looks like there's a huge fight up ahead at the docks."

"Sounds like it, too." She tried to keep her voice steady.

"I've seen every kind of Pure, including fae, and even humans, too. I have no idea what's going on up there."

Bells frowned. "Then why are you going there? We should be going the other direction." She desperately willed him to turn around. He shook his head, though, and kept driving.

Moments later, he yanked the steering wheel hard to the left, tires screeching as the tail drifted. He struggled to control the car but managed to avoid losing control. His voice was as tight as steel wire when he said, "Go back? Not a chance. I'll stop when it gets too dangerous to keep driving, then I'm going out there to take control of this madhouse. You stay in the car, okay? It's enchanted. You'll be safe in here."

What a stupid, rash idea. Prince or no prince, he was probably going to get her killed, but even worse, he would also get himself killed. He seemed to be the only Pure who didn't feel the fae were disposable, so if he got out of the car, she was determined to go with him, no matter how terrifying. The heir to the First Councilor was too important to her people's future for her to passively let his stupidity get him killed.

He slammed on the brakes and the car screeched to a halt, throwing Bells forward hard. "Stay here," he ordered. "The whole dockyards district is in chaos."

With her voice squeaking in fear, Bells said, "If they carry the fighting out of this neighborhood, the whole city could go up."

"There are a lot of dragons here, but they're not fighting together like we're trained. I have to take control if we want to keep this from spreading." He threw the car door open and scrambled out.

She ignored his order to stay put and followed him. He stood motionless as he evaluated the situation. They were on the outskirts of the dock district, but even here, several small groups were engaged in battle. Nearby, two of Jaekob's Guardians stood near overturned motorcycles, battling a cluster of elves. Jaekob pulled his lips back in a snarl and claws grew from his fingertips, four inches long and wickedly sharp. He strode toward his bodyguards, smoke trailing behind him from his nostrils.

Bells ran next to him, still shadow-hidden, and blurted, "You can't go help them. What if something happens to you?"

"Dragons are warriors," he said, and then launched himself into the elves fighting the two dragons. Bells watched as all three dragons began what looked like a perfectly choreographed dance. That was their battle training, she realized, and she watched the deadly fight with mesmerized eyes. Though the elves tried to use their magic before they died, their targets were too nimble. Once Jaekob and his Guardians closed the distance, they tore the elves limb from limb. The elves never had a chance.

When the fight was over, only three seconds later by her count, the dragons stood over the bloody meat laying at their feet, crimson dripping from their claws. She was transfixed, staring in disbelief. She had never seen dragons fight before and suddenly understood with crystal clarity why the dragons, few as they were, stood above all other Pures.

One of the guards shouted, "Sir, you can't be here! It's too dangerous."

Jaekob spat onto the pavement. "I stay. Understood? We have to organize the defenses. If the elves break through the Wards, the whole city will look like this. Split up and go organize the dragons and whatever loyal Pures you can find. We have to push the rioters back."

Both Guardians stared at him for a second, but in the end, they ran toward the fighting by the docks. Jaekob turned to Bells. "I told you to stay in the car. You need to get back there. I can't fight if I'm worried about your safety."

She shook her head. "You can stand here arguing with me or you can save your city. You can't do both because I'm not going back to the car. I'm coming with you. Someone has to make sure you don't do something stupid and get yourself killed."

He laughed, but it was a grim and bitter sound. "What makes you think you can save me? Maybe you didn't see the fight that just happened."

"No, I saw it. As impressive as it was, I saw how reckless you were. You and your Guardians looked like you were in a beautiful, deadly dance, but you can't see everything. You can't look everywhere. I'm coming, so get used to it. I'll be the eyes in the back of your head. Plus, maybe you don't know this, but we fae have more abilities than just talking to plants and hiding."

He shrugged. "You're right—I don't have time to argue with a suicidal fae. Fine, stay here or come. Your fate is your own, though. Don't blame me when someone rips your spine out."

With that, he jogged toward the docks and the raging street battle, and Bells followed.

She sprinted two steps to every one of his as Jaekob booked it through the winding, narrow streets in the dockyard district toward the docks, which was where the worst of the fighting seemed to be. Small fights were going on all over the place—elves fighting weres, weres fighting trolls, even other

Pures attacking unwary fae. Once, Bells saw a group of humans with the "guns" they were so fond of, shooting their noisy weapons into a troll. As they passed each little battle, though, Jaekob kept running and wouldn't stop to help one side or the other.

Panting, Bells asked, "Why aren't you helping these people?"

"No time."

They kept on running.

As they approached an intersection, movement to her left caught her attention and she looked over to see a group of half a dozen elves approaching the intersection, too, running in formation as they headed toward the docks. Jaekob and the elves came to a halt at the same time, no more than 20 feet apart. Jaekob snarled and more smoke rose from his nostrils.

One of the elves in the front, the unit commander, called, "Forward, march."

Jaekob stood his ground. Bells felt her heartbeat rise and struggled against the urge to run. Run-and-hide was the fae way of surviving. Not this time, though; she clenched her fists and bit her lip and stood beside Jaekob.

He held his right hand out, fingers open, and a flash of light burst from his open hand. When it faded, Bells saw he held a sword. It wasn't like the short swords most dragons wore—this one was longer and shaped differently. The word 'scimitar' popped into her mind. Jaekob's scimitar was gorgeous, and she could see runes glowing faintly, etched along the curved blade.

The small elf unit slowed to a halt just outside of striking distance. Then, without any spoken command, they spread out to partially encircle Jaekob and Bells. The elf in charge sneered at Jaekob. "Well, if it isn't the heir. What do you think, boys and girls, will a prince's head fetch a hefty price from the Black Court?"

Jaekob grinned through his snarl. "I don't know, but you'll first have to take it. Why don't you come and try? We'll see if you think it was worth it when we're done."

It was hard to believe these two large, muscular men were busy talking to each other instead of attacking, but Bells didn't mind delaying the inevitable. They weren't going to leave Jaekob without a fight, and she wasn't going to leave him, either.

The elf turned his head a little, staring at Bells. He seemed to lock eyes with her, even though she was shadow-hid. He said, "I see you there, fae. You know the dragons left you to your suffering without even raising a finger to try to help. Why don't you help us, instead? Help your betters and I'll even cut you in on the loot after we deliver his head."

"Why would I join you? Pures are pretty much the only problem we fae have, and this dragon is the only one I've ever seen try to help us, so I think I'll take my chances with him." With her heart pounding so loudly in her ears, she couldn't tell if she'd sounded brave, but she knew how brave she felt. Not very.

"Think about it," the elf said. "With your share, you could buy your family's freedom." He sneered at Jaekob, seemingly expecting Bells to jump him from behind, but his sneer faded a bit when she didn't attack the dragon immediately.

Jaekob had been watching the exchange with a bemused expression but now, holding his sword at the ready, he snarled, "Enough talking. Come take my head if you think you can."

One elf broke ranks and rushed Jaekob. Bells watched in horror as he jumped impossibly high and far, almost like flying. He streaked toward the prince and swung his sword with two hands, upward and diagonally across Jaekob's left side. Amazingly, though, where the elf's sword struck Jaekob, Bells could have sworn he grew thick scales. She couldn't be sure, as they were gone as fast as they'd appeared. While she had heard the sound of metal-on-metal, or scales rather, Jaekob stood uninjured. It was a suicide attack, though, leaving the elf no defense against a counterattack, and Jaekob's scimitar cut the elf nearly in half from shoulder to opposite hip.

"Who's next?" Jaekob asked the remaining elves.

The five became a little more cautious. Swords drawn, they charged all at once. Bells startled at their speed as their swords flashed in and out, but Jaekob was faster. Even so, with five elves swinging against him at once, he couldn't block them all.

Every time one of their swords struck home, Jaekob's scales appeared for just an instant where the blades struck.

Bells had no illusions about what the elves would do once they were done with Jaekob if he lost. It might take them quite a while, but eventually one of them could land a lucky hit. Or they might tire him down enough to slow his swordplay and then they would simply overwhelm him. She had to do something to help.

Looking around frantically for a weapon better than her pocketknife, she saw bits of green growing up through cracks in the pavement. A devious idea came to her and she grinned in spite of her fear. She waved both hands in front of her face, fingers and hands trailing light. Faster and faster, she wove her hands and the light trails merged, getting brighter until they formed one larger symbol. Abruptly, she stopped waving her hands and blew across her palm; the glyph floated quickly toward the elves.

When it drifted into them, it burst apart in a shower of lights. All around the elves, the little bits of green growing up through the pavement stopped being so little—in seconds, they'd grown larger and shot up toward the sky. Behind an elf, one grew into a sapling, and as it grew, its branches folded around him. The branches pinned him and then kept growing, lifting him up. Vines slithered up another elf's legs, around his body, and up to his arms. The vines tightened and held him fast.

The plants grew until all five elves were helpless, and then Jaekob's flashing, slashing blade made short work of them. Panting heavily, he turned toward Bells with his hands on his knees and grunted, "I don't know what you did or how you did it, but it worked. I could have handled them, but...thank you."

Before she could think of a reply, he turned and continued toward the docks. One or two Pures came at him along the way, but he dispatched them easily. No larger groups attacked them.

When they were quite close to the docks, he pointed out a mass of dragons standing side by side as they fought a much larger mob of elves, weres, and trolls. He looked down at her and gave her a grim smile. "Are you ready for this? I suggest you stay out of the way, but if you're going to follow me, stay close. Just don't trip me up."

As he charged into battle, Bells did what she could with her plant magic, but she continually had to use her shadow-walk to avoid attackers. It was impossible to get any spell up to full strength. In the end, though, the dragons defending the docks scattered the mob. The chaos and noise all throughout the dock district seemed to be petering out as well. The battle was won, at least for the moment.

Though his Guardians tried to convince him to leave and go to safety while they mopped up, Jaekob refused, and in the end, there was nothing they could do to force him. "Let's help our wounded," he told them, "and then I can get back to ignoring your advice."

J.A. Culican

Jaekob finished rendering first-aid on the last of the wounded who could be saved just as a dragon flew down to them, summoning his human form as he landed. He walked up to Jaekob and saluted. "Sir, I've scouted the docks district as you ordered."

Jaekob nodded and tossed his bloodied gloves aside. "What news to report?"

Still standing at attention, the scout replied, "It appears as though the Wards held. The dark Pures of the Black Court didn't have the numbers to break through. We don't know why they attacked here, and our only guess why they didn't bring more fighters is that they simply lacked the numbers. Throughout the district, our Guardians have restored order and are now finishing off the wounded attackers and any who refused to run or surrender. The day is won."

While they talked, Bells looked around the plaza. It led to the docks themselves and had been the most heavily warded against the Black Court or dark Pures. She spotted an elf body that lay away from any of the others, and it looked unarmed. She felt a growing concern—something just felt *wrong* about the scene. As she got closer, she saw the elf had no visible wounds and no blood surrounded his body.

While she was examining the elf's body, his clothes begin to wriggle, and by reflex, she stepped back. Moments later, a vine appeared from within his shirtsleeve. There was something blue and pulsing emerging from its tip like tiny electric arcs. She realized in horror that they were thin filaments, more vines growing from the thicker one snaking its way out of his shirtsleeve. The first vine continued to thicken, and before her eyes, the filaments thickened, turning into thin new vines. They were a sickly, electric blue, too, like the first one. His clothes kept squirming and then she saw several more vines began growing out from beneath the dead elf's clothing.

"Jaekob!" she yelled, and even to her own ears, she sounded panicked.

He turned to say something, but whatever it was died on his lips when he saw the body at her feet. He sprinted over. "What in Creation is this?"

A shout sounded behind him and he and Bells both turned to look. The other bodies had also begun growing the thin, pulsing vines. She couldn't see a single corpse that was unaffected. Her first thought was that it was a dragon trap that had taken effect too late, but then the Guardians who fell in battle began to squirm. Moments later, vines began to appear on them, too. Bells felt panic rising. She had never seen anything quite like that, but she had seen something similar when she was very young.

While the vines kept growing and splitting, then growing again, she cried out, "Don't touch them."

Jaekob rolled his eyes. "Why? They're blue vines, and they're only affecting the dead. Don't worry about it." He bent down to the body next to Bells, frowning.

Bells felt her heart skip a beat and she rushed forward, grabbing him. "No. Don't touch it, Jaekob. You'll die."

He stopped and stood straight again. "Whatever for? It's only on the dead, and I'm not dead."

"Not yet. It's a fungus. Not like any I've seen before, but trust me—you don't want to touch that."

A Guardian said, "I'll do it, sir. I have gloves on."

Jaekob nodded and the Guardian reached down to flip the body over. Then he and Bells recoiled, backing up a step. The elf's entire front side was melting into a truly disgusting black-and-red goo. Only Jaekob stood still. "He's decomposing right before our eyes."

Bells nodded. She had worried about a fungus and now she was pretty sure the vines were mycorrhizal strands. She turned to the Guardian, whipping her head around, and blurted, "How do you feel?"

"I feel fine," he said, shrugging with his hands out to either side. Then he cocked his head and looked down at his right glove, a confused look on his face. Then to his left glove. "What the..."

Thin, blue tendrils, each only as thick as a hair, had begun winding their way around the gloves, splitting and multiplying. It looked almost fractal.

The Guardian quickly flung off his gloves. "By Creation, what is it?"

Jaekob frowned but didn't answer right away. At last, he said, "I think I see. *This* is the real attack. This is how they intended to get through the Wards, but we stopped the elves. It was a matter of inches."

"Um, sir?" the Guardian said, his voice shaking. One blue tendril snaked from his wrist and up his arm.

He hadn't removed his glove fast enough. Jaekob stripped off the man's shirt and drew his sword, ready to chop his arm off to save his life. Arms could grow back if you were a dragon. But as he drew back his sword, he froze. The man's veins and arteries were visible through his skin, a deep blue pattern already reaching the man's shoulder and growing up his neck.

The Guardian began to scream, whether from fear or pain she couldn't tell. Probably both. He fell to the ground and began twitching, blue foam coming from his mouth.

Jaekob took a step toward him but Bells grabbed him. "Get back," she said, dragging him away. Quickly, she threw a fungus repellent spell toward the guard. The Guardian coughed, splattering blue froth all around him. "If that had landed on you..."

"Yeah, I get it. That poor man. But look, *all* the bodies are getting overrun by these things. And they're spreading." Jaekob snarled, his eyes flaring red. "The elves will pay for this."

Bells nodded and said, "Yes, of course. But right now, we have more important things to worry about. We have to find a cure, and fast. We have the outbreak contained to the docks for now, but for how long?"

Jaekob took a deep breath. "Damn. Fine. You fae are the best at this, right? We'll need fae to fix this mess the elves started."

Bells nodded. She had saved the Dragon Prince, not once but twice that day. It felt good to be a protector, even if only for a little while.

The day dragged on as Jaekob rallied the docks district until the dragons had restored some semblance of order. Those who were infected were sent—at spear-point, if necessary—to a horrid area where the dead also were slowly being collected. Dragons air-dropped stacks of tarps so the survivors could safely move the bodies, but each body took two tarps—one to roll the body onto and the other to carry the corpse back. This made it possible to move corpses at all, though two fae still were lost during the effort after accidentally touching an infected body while moving it.

There wasn't much Bells could do since Jaekob had things under as much control as possible, given the circumstances, so she spent the afternoon being his messenger. She hadn't wanted to leave his side, but as he pointed out, he had enough Guardians who could protect him, and he sent two with her, as well, despite her protests that the Guardians would only make her more visible.

Running back and forth left her a lot of time to think. Mostly, she thought about her family. She missed them, and it was possible she'd never see them again. What if the fungus became airborne? How many spores did it take to become infected? Her father would be the most crushed of her family if she died here today.

On the other hand, Jaekob had saved her family from the troll and from her village foreman. Maybe it would cost her life but she was at peace with that if her family was safe. Coming to the city in the first place had been a terrible risk and she'd been mentally prepared for the worst before she ever got to Philadelphia.

When she got back to Jaekob after her latest run and handed him messages written on slips of paper, he looked exhausted. She felt wiped out, too, actually, but his exhaustion was plain even in his voice, which was hoarse and had a little tremble. His back was stooped, shoulders slumped, and he had dark circles under his eyes.

He smiled when he saw her and took the paper slips. "You look exhausted, Bells. Why don't you take a nap? We don't know how long we'll be here."

She closed her eyes and felt sleep rushing at her, even standing up. He had a point. "Yes, you might be right," she said, suddenly eager to fall asleep somewhere quiet. "But you're more tired than I am. Leave this to your Guardians for a while and come rest with me. I'm not going if you don't."

After a long pause, he said, "Yeah... Yes, of course. You need sleep. If you won't catch some rest without me, then for your sake, I'll go with you."

Bells suppressed a smirk and saw the nearest Guardian smile wanly. She said, "It's a deal. Thanks. Who knows what kind of protection I'll need here in this mess. People can get dangerous when cornered like this."

Actually, that was true, and as they trudged toward a nearby empty building, she found that she really was glad to have a dragon with her.

Bells awoke suddenly and looked around, half-panicked, but it was only Jaekob. He was standing at the building's one small window, looking out and muttering under his breath.

"What's wrong?" she asked, her tongue not yet working quite right as she came awake.

He rubbed his eyes with his palms. "Ugh. We've been asleep for an hour and a half. I told them to wake me after half an hour. Now I'm more tired than when I went to sleep."

"I'm sure they were just doing their duty for you, the Prince of Dragons." She sent her senses outward as far as she could, though, and didn't relax until she felt the energies of living beings. Just in case the reason they hadn't woken him was that they had all died. It was a mighty relief, for once, to feel people all around.

Jaekob smiled down at her, and with his rumpled hair and cheesy grin, he looked even more handsome than before in a natural sort of way. He reached down to help her up, and the feel of his strong hand on hers was entirely too pleasant. She cleared her mind of the thought. He was a dragon and she was fae. A nice daydream, though.

"Come on, little fae," he said, still smiling a little. "We have to go see how far they got in moving the bodies while we wasted the day away."

When they stepped outside, she saw from the sun's position that he was right. They had slept for almost two hours, actually. They walked side by side back to the work area. When they arrived, a Guardian approached, glancing back and forth between them, but his expression didn't reveal his thoughts. "Sir, we've finished moving the dead away from the water and out of the buildings where some crawled off to die. It was hard work and everyone's worn out, but the job is done. The city is safe from contagion."

Jaekob took a handful of paper slips the Guardian held out and skimmed through them. "Excellent," he said when he got to the last slip. "You've outdone yourself. You shouldn't have let me sleep, though. My place is leading, not sleeping while everyone else does the work."

Bells looked at him in surprise. She simply hadn't expected a dragon to say such a thing. Weren't they all lazy and vicious? No—that was what the elves told her people, nothing more. She looked at the Guardian to see if he seemed surprised by Jaekob's words, but no, he just kept giving his brief description of the big picture situation. Maybe there was more to Jaekob than being a killing machine. She filed that away to think on later.

A were approached and the conversation died. He stopped just out of striking distance and politely bowed his head. "Jaekob, one of the elves here got a brief message, by spell, from elves outside the docks district. The first cases of this strange disease have popped up on the other side of your Wards, but they've been quarantined."

A shadow passed over them all and Bells looked up. A large, green dragon circled above, wings spread wide as it slowed itself to land. She nudged him and pointed. "Jaekob, a dragon is coming down."

"I see it. I imagine he has new instructions for what to do here, from the Dragon Council." He stepped away from the group and waited for the newcomer to land, then the two spoke in hushed tones with their heads together.

Bells couldn't hear what they said, even extending her senses. The other dragon must have worn a privacy screen pendant or something. She had a hard time standing still as she waited.

A couple minutes later, Jaekob came back and said, "The situation is grim. Confirmation that the disease is spreading beyond the docks, for one. Worse, it's spreading faster than anyone can do anything about, though they're trying to quarantine the infected."

Bells' eyes went wide. "So what do we do about it?" she asked, trying not to let her voice tremble. The thought of a city that big being overrun by the weird and deadly disease, well, it was staggering.

Jaekob shook his head and scratched his neck. "Well, the Dragon Council needs to come up with a new plan of action, and the First Councilor has ordered me to return home to help them. I'd fly there but they just put up a new boundary, another shell farther out than the Wards, to slow the spread."

"Oh no. How do we get in?"

"We'll have to walk in. Come on." He began to walk toward the city proper, then paused and turned back to the Guardian. "Stay on top of these people, keep them calm, and send regular reports to the Guardians at the Wards gateway. It's due west. Just take the biggest road going that direction and you'll find it."

The dragon saluted, and Jaekob put his hand on Bells' back. "Let's get you out of here—you and my bodyguards."

She took a deep breath. Part of her wanted to stay and help the people stuck inside the shell but she wasn't going to let Jaekob out of her sight until she absolutely had to. She needed to know what was going on and Jaekob was the only way she'd learn the truth. "Lead on."

They headed west with four Guardians flanking them on all sides, alert for danger. It took only about fifteen minutes to find the shell gate—a gap between two trees, heavily guarded—and Jaekob walked up to the Guardians blocking it. "Let us pass. I have business with the Dragon Council," he said almost casually. His tone was the same one she used when coaxing plants to grow—like it was inconceivable they wouldn't just do what he asked.

"Negative, my prince." The Guardian in front checked a clipboard. "My orders are to let you out, but no one else is listed, sir."

Jaekob snarled. "I'm not some random Pure. I gave you an order, Dragon. Step aside, while you still can and let us through."

Bells found herself taking an involuntary step back from him. Either he was very used to being obeyed or he was tired enough to be dangerous. Or more likely, both.

The guard immediately got down on one knee, bowed his head, and put his fist over his heart. Still looking down, he said, "Forgive me, my prince, but the orders come from the Dragon Council and are signed by the First Councilor. Only you may come through, and you are instructed to report to the Council. With respect, sir."

Bells felt her throat tighten and bit her lip, hoping the pain would keep her from panicking. Jaekob was going to leave her there, and she'd be left in a chaotic city district without any protection, unable to escape the creeping death inside it.

Jaekob was silent for a painfully long moment until he said, "Then I regret to inform the Council I am unable to obey their instructions. These are also my people and I won't leave them to risk infection here by themselves, alone and forgotten. Let Mikah lead his people. Please pass along my sincerest regrets, Guardian."

He turned and strode away from the gateway, leaving the rest of them to stare at each other in surprise. Suddenly, Bells felt even more frightened than she had before. If he died in there with her, no one would help the fae. She scrambled after him and his Guardians ran with her.

Then, from behind, she heard the gate guard yelling, "My prince, please stop! I have a message from your father giving you authorization."

Jaekob stopped suddenly. He turned around slowly and Bells could have sworn he winked at her right before he strode back toward the gate. "And what is this message? I'd have thought you'd pass that on to me when I arrived here. Explain yourself."

Bells suppressed a mischievous grin at Jaekob's tone of voice, but the guard turned two shades lighter. Only Jaekob's wink told her he was messing with the poor guy. Still, he really should have given Jaekob all of the information.

The guard abruptly stood ramrod straight—any soldier's natural defense against getting in trouble, from what Bells had seen over the years—and said, "My prince, your personal authorization did not include other people. We have orders to quarantine the docks. But the First Councilor's instructions did say to get you out of the area 'at all costs.' Sir, this

Guardian was only trying to accomplish all his duties, sir."

Jaekob chuckled and put his arm over the guard's shoulders. In a quiet, conspiratorial tone, he said, "Don't worry about it. It's not your fault you have conflicting orders. Sheesh, commanders—am I right?"

The guard's eyes flicked all over the place, a sure sign of nervousness. Probably wondering if it were a ruse before Jaekob let the hammer fall right on him. "Yes, sir... I mean, no, they're doing what they can, I'm sure—"

"Um, 'this Guardian?'" Jaekob said, smirking.

"... This Guardian is sure?"

Jaekob gave the guard a slight squeeze, then let him go. In a much louder voice designed to carry, he said, "Well done, Guardian. Your dedication to duty is hereby noted. If contacted again, please let the Council know I'll be there when I can, and that I, too, have duties to perform."

The guard swallowed hard, twice, but saluted smartly. "Yes, sir."

Jaekob led Bells and his guards through the gate and into the unaffected areas of the city. She felt an irresistible urge to keep looking at him when she thought he wasn't watching, trying to evaluate the new facets of his personality. The Prince of Dragons, heir to the First Councilor of the mightiest race on Earth or beyond the Veil, had just risked his life rather than leave her or his bodyguards behind. He valued their lives enough to risk his own.

So why had he done nothing to help the fae? She followed him into the city, feeling very conflicted and confused.

J.A. Culican

When they had gone only about twenty steps beyond the gate, they rounded a street corner and Bells stopped abruptly, mouth gaping as she stared at the scene before her. Jaekob, too, had frozen in place. It was just too surreal not to stare. The entire time Bells had been in Philadelphia, the streets had been busy. Far busier than her village, at least. Now, however, only a few intrepid souls wandered the streets and they all walked quickly as though attending to urgent business. Bits of trash blew around the streets, which might have been common in some city zones but was unheard of in modern

Philadelphia so close to the market. Important people, people with money, were the kind who usually traveled that particular street, and they had no interest in seeing trash. The Pures usually had dedicated crews of fae cleaners in the area, keeping everything tidy.

That day, she saw no cleaners and very few people of any kind

"What is on their faces?" Jaekob asked.

Bells squinted her eyes to try to see better but couldn't tell. She had never seen anything quite like it. It was as though every person had half their face erased.

One of the Guardians said, "They appear to be wearing face masks, sir. Protection from the fungus."

As the only fae in the group, Bells knew better than anyone there that a simple face mask wouldn't stop an airborne fungus. She said, "No, I mean... Yes, that's probably why they're wearing those things, but if this fungus somehow gets airborne, the masks won't help. It'll still get in their eyes."

Jaekob let out a low growl and then said, "One of my Guardians got infected just by allowing the fungus to touch his skin, remember? He even had clothes on when he touched the infected body. It infected his gloves."

Bells shuddered. It was a terrifying thought and an even worse memory.

Jaekob made a beeline toward a man across the street, an elf in rather fancy-looking clothes. The moment he noticed Jaekob approaching, he practically jumped to the other side of the sidewalk, as far away as he could get. "Get away from me. I don't know you and I can't help you." He began to jog away, leaving a stunned Jaekob in his wake. When he was safely past any chance of being intercepted, he glanced over his shoulder and shouted, "Put a mask on, for Creation's sake. You're probably already infected, stupid dragon."

Jaekob walked back, shaking his head in disbelief. "I have no idea what's going on."

After they had walked another half a block, an elf woman wearing a face mask like the rest stepped off the curb and fell. It looked like half her leg disappeared and Bells realized she must have stepped into a deep pothole. Even from her distance, she heard a loud *crack* and the woman let out a terrible scream.

Bells strode toward the injured woman but a fae man going the other direction passed by the fallen elf, who held her arm outstretched toward him and cried for help. He roared at the woman with his fists clenched, leaning forward like he might strike her. Bells stopped, unable to believe her eyes. He ran from the woman, turned a corner, and sprinted out of sight.

From right behind Bells, Jaekob asked, "What on earth is going on here?"

She could only shake her head.

A Guardian said, "If a fae man feels brave enough to scream at an elf, I can't imagine the level of fear there must be in the city."

Jaekob nodded, thinking. His voice sounded hesitant when he said, "Here is what we know. Everyone who can stay inside or hidden is doing so. Those who have to go outside wear face masks and avoid everyone they see. They're fearful enough that they won't even help someone injured in the middle of the street, not even fae. People must think it might be airborne, but we know that it isn't."

"No, not yet," Bells confirmed. "It only spreads by those tendrils, those disgusting, pulsing, vine-looking things. Those couldn't get through the Wards."

"But we don't know whether this is happening everywhere in the city or just here next to the dockyards neighborhood."

"Why don't you summon your dragon forms and fly out?" Bells asked. "If you head toward your house, you'll be able to see what's going on all over the city, and I can just meet you there as quickly as I can."

Jaekob looked up at the sky, shaking his head. "First, I won't leave you here like this. It's my fault you're in this situation in the first place. Just as importantly, though, look up. What do you see?"

Curious, Bells looked up and scanned the sky, looking for whatever could possibly keep a dragon grounded. "I don't see anything. Just some small groups of dragons flying around. Obviously, dragons aren't afraid of flying."

One of the Guardians chuckled but Jaekob cut him off with a slash of his hand through the air before turning back to Bells. His expression softened. "Those aren't just little groups of dragons. Those are half-wings, basically half a squad of soldiers. They're flying in formation and they're the only ones in the air. I'm willing to bet they have orders to ground or even flame anyone in the air who isn't in uniform, in formation, and on duty."

"Are you serious? Why would they keep everyone grounded? The fungus isn't airborne. They should let the healthy people get out, right?"

"If only it were that simple," Jaekob replied. "They must know how contagious it is. Both the Dragon Council and the White King's people are afraid enough to lock everyone down in the city. I guarantee you all the ways in and out of the city are being guarded, as well."

Bells had no reply. She took a deep breath and looked up into the sky, blinking rapidly and wishing she had never come back to Philadelphia. But what was done couldn't be undone and she had to make the best of it. At least her present companion was a powerful dragon, guarded by even more of his kind. For the moment, he wasn't willing to leave her behind, so she was as safe as any fae could expect to be. For now. "Well, I think we should—"

She felt a tugging sensation in the back of her mind, almost overlooked and yet impossible to completely ignore, much like when the dinner bell rang while she was hypnotized by the repetitive boredom of weaving fabric.

"What is it?" Jaekob asked. She heard a tinge of worry in his voice with the way his pitch rose on the last syllables.

She couldn't remember what she'd been about to say—the sensation had been such a surprise—so she shook her head. "I don't know. I felt like someone grabbed a loose thread at the back of my brain and pulled hard. Like, unraveling my mind for a second. It kicked out every other thought."

He shrugged and went back to looking around for danger as he said, "Telepathy. You've never been contacted before?"

"No... It's not a fae thing."

A Guardian smiled down at her. "Of course it is. Just rare in your kind. Usually, it runs in families. The connection gets stronger if you're related."

Bells frowned. What relative did she know with telepathy? She couldn't think of any. Yet that tug had been plenty strong. "Well, it's gone now. A mystery, I guess."

Jaekob's barking laughter surprised her and brought heat into her cheeks. He said, "No mystery. You just didn't answer. They really don't teach you this stuff as a kid, I see. When you feel that, you have to... I don't know, like, open your mind up. You have to accept the call by lowering your ego, that sense of yourself that makes you separate from the world and from the caller."

Bells grimaced. "Humans do that. Cut themselves off. Pures, and fae especially, are all about being open to the world around them."

"Not like this," Jaekob replied. "I mean, you have to *forget* yourself, forget you're a separate person. When you talk telepathically, you stop being separate. With training, you can block some things off and still be open, but at first, whoever you talk to will see everything there is to see, assuming they know what to look for."

Well. That sure didn't sound like fun. There were some things she didn't want anyone to know, she realized as she looked at Jaekob. Still, the timing was too weird to be a coincidence. "It has to be related to this fungus thing or whatever is going on here. The first time anyone tries to crawl inside my head with me, and it's in the middle of all this?"

Jaekob's mouth tightened, lips thinning. "You have a point. If it happens again, I think you should let them in."

As they again started walking toward his house, safely within the Wards, Bells waited for another tug at her brain-thread, but it didn't come. Yet, if it were important, she wondered whether she could afford not to know what it had been about. She let her mind go quiet as their feet stepped rhythmically on the pavement, using the steady beat to lull herself into a blank state. Then she reached out, not with her senses, as usual, but with her thoughts, seeking that thread that had tried to connect with hers.

She had no idea what she was doing, so when she felt the tug in her mind again, it almost startled her out of her blank state. A familiar-sounding voice came to mind and she wondered whether it was her imagination, but then the words became stronger, more clear.

"You aren't imagining it. You're in danger out there."

"No kidding." Everything about the neighborhood they walked through screamed danger.

"That's what I said, kiddo. Listen, I—"

Who in Creation's eyes was she talking to?

"You don't recognize the voice?"

It seemed disappointed.

"Well, we only met once. This is Hawking. The family bond is the only way I found you out there since we've never melded before."

Melded... That would be the merging Jaekob had mentioned. Oh no, too late—did they catch that? She felt her heartbeat rise.

"Calm down or you'll break the meld. This is hard, you know, since you aren't trained. Don't

worry about Jaekob. He's a dragon, you're a fae. You have actual things to worry about."

Bells frowned and had the urge to deny whatever he was suggesting, but part of her feared the response, so instead, she shoved the thoughts away and did her best to simply focus and receive the message as clearly as she could.

"That's better. Much better, in fact. Listen, you can't go back to Jaekob's manor. I saw that's where you're headed. And you need to bring him with you. Only a friendly dragon can help us, now. I failed to stop it, so now I have to help that dragon."

Bells felt a sensation of fiery anger with the incoming thought. She wondered—

"Stop. No time for questions. I have a group of people you need to take him to. They will help. Trust me. It's the only hope any of us have, in the long run."

Odd. Bells wasn't sure how she felt about luring Jaekob to meet a secret group of Hawking's people. Hadn't he been part of the plot to kill the First Councilor? In fact, she remembered with her own rising anger, he'd used her to do it. She couldn't trust him, not with Jaekob's life.

"He's dead anyway if you don't listen. Listen! Yes, they tried to kill Mikah, but they failed. And now, the plan has changed."

"Right. Changed to setting off some sort of plague and killing—"

"We didn't have anything to do with the contagion that is just starting to run through the city, but we have to stop it. These people you need to meet, they know what to do. They have a plan. If you don't trust me, trust that the five dragon warriors with you can handle a simple secret meeting."

Before she had a chance to think of a response, an image flooded her mind. Not just into it, but rather, she felt a physical pain. It was like information was burning itself into her brain. It came as an image of a corner with two street signs in front of a plain-looking house with brass street numbers plainly visible. But the pain was overwhelming and she felt her knees buckle. All she could see was the image of that house, but she felt strong arms catch her as she fell and gently set her on the ground with her head resting on something soft.

"It did burn itself into your brain. That's how brains and memories work. You'll never forget it, not for a long time at least. Go there. Save the city. Maybe even more, if this infection escapes Philadelphia—"

The voice in her head vanished in an instant, leaving her mind reeling to decipher what was in her head and what was real for a couple of seconds. She heard Jaekob's voice, loud and strong. "Bells, wake up. Where are you? Come back."

She blinked rapidly and the real world replaced whatever mental zone she'd been in and the house's image. "We have somewhere to be, and there's no time to lose."

She got to her feet and began walking away from his manor, finding it odd that she remembered exactly how to get from a place she'd never been to another place she'd never been. Hawking would have to answer some questions someday, when all this was behind them.

Bells led them unerringly toward the house. Jaekob had been hesitant at first, but as she pointed out, it couldn't hurt. If someone had an idea to fix things, they'd be foolish not to at least hear it out, maybe even negligent. That was when he gritted his teeth, nodded, and held out his hand for her to lead the way.

The path took them out of the neighborhood right outside the docks district into a less wealthy area. Some of the houses were burned, others abandoned, but many look occupied. Elves and dragons wouldn't likely be the ones to call this place home, and that left weres, trolls, and maybe some of the wealthier fae.

She hoped it would be fae who awaited them.

Two hours after she got the message, she saw the house up ahead. It looked exactly as it did in her memory, which was both surprising and not surprising at all. Hawking had lain the path so clearly, she would have been more surprised if it hadn't been an exact match. Cousin Hawking must have been there before, which only raised her hopes that wealthy fae might be waiting for her.

"Wait," Jaekob said, the first time he'd spoken since they began the trip. "It could be dangerous." He turned to his Guardians and picked two. "Go inspect the area. Fly, if you have to, but fly low. I don't want anyone getting burned up by the sky patrol."

Bells watched as they carefully inspected virtually the entire block's worth of houses surrounding their target, then checked the house itself. One Guardian did fly, but only about twenty feet up, and he landed right away when a half-wing of air patrol Dragons dove at him from above; once he landed, the other dragons flew back up. The warning was clear.

When they returned some twenty minutes later, they reported everything looked clear, but they'd seen people inside watching them through the curtains.

"So, they know we're here," Jaekob muttered. Louder, he asked, "Did they make any aggressive moves?"

"No, sir. But there are definitely more than two people inside."

Bells frowned. Enough was enough. "Of course they know we're here. Whoever sent that message," she said, carefully avoiding Hawking's name—she didn't know if he'd escaped or been let loose—"must have told them I was coming. We're wasting time we don't have."

Jaekob grinned at her, both surprising and a little thrilling. He had a rather nice smile... "Well then, let's go. Two guards on you, two on me. Stay close together, just in case, but keep your weapons sheathed. We won't make any aggressive moves unless they do it first."

The Guardians saluted, then formed up around her and Jaekob. She took a deep breath before heading for the front door. Jaekob muttered something the entire way, but Bells spent the time sending her senses outward, directed at the house. The Guardians had been right, there were more than two people inside. Six, in fact, and four were fae. The other two were a were and an elf, which immediately made her nervous.

The guards drew even closer to their two charges as Bells relayed the new information. Then they headed to the building. As she walked up the three creaky wooden steps leading to the patio, the front door opened a crack. She caught the glint of a door chain—it wouldn't have stopped a dragon.

A man stood, obscured by shadow inside, peering out the door. "Just you two. No guards."

Jaekob let out a laugh that somehow sounded both brave and insulting, but was there a hint of nervous bravado she caught in his tone? He said, "I'll not be trusting either of our lives to your good intentions. The guards come in or we leave."

Bells blurted, "But—"

The man inside interrupted, talking loudly over her, "And if you leave, the city dies. Make up your mind. If you don't come in, this group will leave Philadelphia and this horrible world to you all, and head back through the Veil to hide until it kills that world, too."

"Impossible!" Bells said, without thinking first. No one could go back through the Veil until both the Crown of Pures and the Black Court signed an accord in blood, and that would only happen after a long and terrible war, when both sides were too wiped out to keep fighting over the magic that poured through Earth's ley line veins.

"Wrong," the man said. "There are ways. We're not sharing those with anyone else, much less you people. It doesn't matter what you believe, though. If you leave, we aren't going to try to stop you. We won't even care. We're only doing this to save our brethren. If you let us, that is."

Bells turned to Jaekob. He looked uncertain, shifting his weight subtly from one foot to the other again and again. Actually, he looked like he was about to either run away or charge through the door. Adrenaline did that to people. She felt it herself. "Fine. I'm going in," she said to the man without taking her eyes off Jaekob. Looking into his eyes, she said, "Are you coming? Either way, I can't just walk away without even trying to save the people in this city. There are fae here, you know, and dragons."

Jaekob nodded and his eyes narrowed. "Guardians, post up outside. One at each corner, so you can see one another. If anyone tries to leave before we do, burn them all. Is that understood?"

The Guardians saluted, then marched away to take up their positions, though the glances they gave their leader told Bells they weren't happy about leaving Bells and Jaekob alone on the porch. She suddenly felt rather exposed. "So, let us in and tell us what you need."

The door opened and a middle-aged fae poked his head out, looking left and right. He wore a basic, brown tweed suit. For a fae to wear any kind of suit, he had to be wealthy by their standards. Satisfied no one was lurking beside the door, he nodded and opened it all the way. "Come in."

Jaekob pressed his arm against Bells' chest, just below her collarbone, holding her back. He stepped through first. It was amazing that a dragon would go in first when a mere fae farm girl was right there to take the plunge. There wasn't time to dwell on it, though, so she came in on his heels.

The house was pretty much what she'd expected, though fairly large for a human home. It had furniture that looked well made yet only moderately expensive. Around an L-shaped couch and two love seats sat five people, all facing a granite coffee table. There were six when the tweed-suited fae sat down.

Bells sat on the only empty love seat and Jaekob simply stood behind her rather than coming around to sit next to her. She felt his presence. His aura was red with sparkling-blue strands running through it. Angry but hiding it well, and confident. Cocky, even.

"Well," Jaekob said, "you went to a lot of trouble to get us here. You'd better have a good reason."

The tweed-suited man's gaze locked onto Jaekob unflinchingly. He said, "I'm Dawning, and I don't recall inviting you here at all. Bells is the one our mutual associate invited."

Bells recoiled, imagining all sorts of worst-case scenarios. She was shocked that a fae would talk to a dragon in such a way, but a glance at the other Pures around the table showed that they, too, were staring at Jaekob without flinching. She was also surprised that it was a fae who led the group, not the elf. She wanted to ask why Dawning led the conversation, but she froze as she waited for Jaekob's response.

Thankfully, he chuckled instead of tearing the room apart. He said, "I've known Bells for longer than I've known any of you. I won't leave her alone in here with you." His voice was steady and even, dripping with unbending resolve. His reaction was just one of several surprises at that table, apparently.

Dawning looked around at the other Pures and raised his hand, finger outstretched indicating Jaekob. "What shall we do about this uninvited guest? We all know who he is. The heir to the First Councilor, who rules the city and arguably the world, yet he does nothing to stop the war. This so-called prince sits in luxury while the other people of the Veil suffer. To create peace, dragons have always prepared for war, but they've abandoned their duties as warriors. *They've abandoned us.* I say this dragon can't be trusted. Shall we remove him before we bring Bells into our confidence? Who can trust a dragon who is afraid to fight?"

Bells froze, waiting for Jaekob to lash out. If these people attacked him, they would be mighty surprised at which side she joined. But Jaekob let him finish his speech and then seconds ticked by without any response. She looked over her shoulder and saw Jaekob picking at his fingernails. He was the picture of disinterest. So, he had been more honest than she realized when he said the only reason he was there was for her safety, and it was obvious he didn't intend to make a case for himself to stay—he just wasn't going to leave. In a way, that made sense because he still wasn't in that fight. The dragons under Mikah had stayed out of it all, despite Awakening early because of the war.

Well, if he wasn't going to stand up for himself, she would. She wasn't about to go anywhere with these people or trust their intentions, not without Jaekob. If he left, she would too. She made a snap decision and practically jumped to her feet, facing the other Pures. "Jaekob is to be trusted. If you don't trust him, then how can I trust you?" She shook her head.

"How can you say that?" Dawning asked. "Hawking gave you instructions on how to meet the dragon in the first place. For his efforts, the dragons had their secret police haul him from his house in broad daylight. He would still be imprisoned under the dragons' not-so-tender mercies if it weren't for the plague spreading across the city, diverting their attention. Even with that, Hawking barely made it out. And yet, even knowing you're friends with this... this dragon... Hawking still tried to save your life by sending you to us. He did it so we might work together to save everyone."

Jaekob still didn't reply, and Bells saw mostly boredom in his aura. He already had his say and apparently felt there was nothing more to add.

Well, she wasn't done standing up for him since he wouldn't stand up for himself. "Hawking was arrested because it seemed clear he was involved in your conspiracy to assassinate Mikah. The timing was rather conspicuous. Don't try to deny you're involved in that."

Dawning let his hands drop to his sides and shook his head. "We had nothing to do with that.

You must have suspected it or you wouldn't be here. Mikah has many enemies. They simply spotted an opportunity and tried to take advantage of it. Or did you miss seeing how poorly organized they were?"

Bells had to admit they had a point. It was a terribly executed attempt at assassination. Perhaps even the dragons thought Hawking wasn't involved—otherwise, they would have killed him, or at least they certainly wouldn't have allowed him to escape.

She said, "Let's just assume for a moment that what you say is true and you're being honest when you say that your ultimate goal is peace. From what I've seen, the dragons want nothing more than that. Why do you think they haven't gotten involved? I say it's because the Pures are fighting amongst themselves. The Dragon Awakening wasn't because of yet another Earthling human war. Maybe I'm wrong, but have you ever known dragons to be cowards? I haven't seen any cowards among them, I promise you that. So what do you want, peace? Action? Or do you just want to sit here and talk about doing something?"

She felt a bolt like lightning run down her spine. She had done it! She, Bells, nothing but the fae daughter of a farmer, had just stood up to an elder. And not one but six, including an elf and a were. A week ago, she never would have even considered standing up to these people.

The other Pures shifted in their seats. Bells saw them exchanging glances and realized they were possibly talking amongst themselves telepathically. Well, she wasn't going to back down. She kept her eyes locked on Dawning's, practically daring him to contradict her. And if they all rushed at Jaekob, they were in for quite a surprise. She had seen him in action, and he was no run-of-the-mill Guardian. And Guardians were pretty much the best warriors in the world.

After several seconds of silence, she was done waiting. She stood and stepped beside the love seat—coincidentally giving Jaekob a clear line of fire at the group, if needed—and said, "If you really want peace, you couldn't get a more powerful ally than the heir to the First Councilor. I've wondered why

Jaekob came into my life when he did, and why I came to Philadelphia when I did."

The elf made a hissing, spitting noise, then said, "Creation made us and then left us to our own will. That is what matters, not some imagined destiny."

"Elves may not believe in predestination, but we fae believe Creation causes everything to happen for a reason. Either way, though, if you really want peace, Jaekob could be the only one who can make it happen. So, why don't you quit wasting time our people don't have, and just tell us why you brought us here."

Dawning had listened to her patiently, without interrupting. He began to nod his head slowly, as though thinking about Bells' words carefully. At last, he said, "If this dragon will follow you where you need to go, we have decided that your words have merit. You're right, Creation does lead us to where we need to be and when we need to be there. This can't be a coincidence. On that note, I have something important to tell you."

Bells clenched her jaw. Well, of course they did. It couldn't be as simple as showing up, shaking hands, and declaring the problem solved. "Yeah, why else would you have gone to such trouble to bring us here? I'm here of my own free will, or at Creation's guidance—who knows which? So please, just tell me what I need to know. If it'll save lives, I'll do it."

She sensed Jaekob's aura turn a cool, cerulean shade of blue; he had suddenly tensed, listening carefully and yet pretending not to. She was beginning to get frustrated. She focused on Dawning, though, and waited for some sort of answer as she tried to rally her patience.

Dawning nodded his head toward the other Pures. "If you please?"

The elf stood. His robe was made of the finest printed silks, and silver and gold threads were woven into it to create subtle patterns. He was clearly wealthy. "Let me tell you a story. It's short, yet it has a very long history. It starts with a sword. The only one in the world like it, this was a very special weapon of war, created beyond the memory of any living being. It is a sword of war, preordained at the dawn of Creation to bring peace to the world."

J.A. Culican

Bells frowned as she listed to the elf's tale. He said the sword was named *Shmsharatsh*, the Sword of Fire. The original legends, first written down in ancient Egypt, said it came from ancient Persia, but the sword was far, far older than those first records. None knew who forged it, but it was supposedly predestined to save the world. Or save the world from itself, depending on the translation.

At the end, Dawning said, "Those of us in the Sword Society have guarded it throughout history, keeping it hidden from those who would use it to rule the world. When the Germans found it during their second great war, the last time you dragons were Awakened, we had to move it for the first time in over a thousand years. The safest place we could find was in a relatively new nation which rose to great power after that second German war."

Jaekob chuckled. "America? Seriously? I find it hard to believe this fearsome weapon is here in this land."

Dawning ignored Jaekob and kept his eyes locked on Bells. "The sword is powerful, and only one with a good heart could ever be trusted with it."

Jaekob slammed his fist on the love seat's arm. "Enough. Bells, I will be outside when you're done listening to fables and conspiracy theories. Don't be long, though. We have a city to save, and that's not going to happen sitting on a couch in some fae's living room."

Bells' eyes narrowed, but he was already walking out. She let him go without arguing. That comment about "some fae"... Not very nice, all things considered.

Dawning grunted. "Well. That comes as no surprise. An arrogant dragon, who would have thought it? None of us expected we'd get anything more from him than to meet our minimum expectations."

Turning back to Dawning, Bells replied, "This does sound far-fetched, though. More importantly, *why are you telling me this?* I'm going back to my farm in a bit, where I'll raise up crops, not swords. We're not even allowed to carry anything bigger than a kitchen knife, so there's that. I'd never get my foreman's permission to wander off on some fool's quest for a sword no one has heard of and which I can't carry legally anyway."

"Legally? What are you, a human? You—"

"I'm not going to get myself killed to retrieve some old sword for you." Bells stared him in the eyes, unflinching.

Dawning looked down and let out a long, slow breath. When he looked back up, he said, "You are the only person Hawking trusts for this. We trust him. It has to be you to get the *Shmsharatsh.* If you don't, this infection will swallow Philadelphia and then the world. Believe me."

Bells curled her lip back into a snarl. "If it's so important that you Sword Society folks have kept it safe all this time, why don't *you* go get it? It's absurd. This is a trap, right? Payback for reporting Nigel, my village foreman. I want no part of it."

"The world will be destroyed, Bells, and you with it."

She felt dire warning bells ringing in the back of her mind at his words. "Then go get it," she said in a flurry. "You know where it is. What's the problem?"

"It's you who don't see the problem," Dawning said, shifting in his seat, jaw clenched.

The elf, who had yet to give his name, said, "Dawning, just tell her. She won't go without it. If she still says no, we can just wipe this meeting out of her memories and send her off to die with everyone else, on her farm, among her family."

Dawning snarled, "That knowledge is not to be given to outsiders. In all these thousands of years—"

The elf interrupted, "—there has never been a surer sign of the time of flames."

Bells glanced around the room, measuring the others' reactions. Dawning stared hard at the floor, frozen. The other fae and the were exchanged glances, but none spoke up to argue against the elf's idea.

At last, Dawning drew a deep breath and let it out slowly, his jaw muscles relaxing again. He nodded once, curtly, then looked at Bells. "Very well. I'll tell you what you ask to know, though you are not a member of the Sword Society."

Bells felt a shiver run across her scalp. The situation suddenly seemed less amusing and more frightening. Legends. Secret societies bigger than just the conspirators in that room. An ancient doomsday weapon. She waited expectantly, barely daring to breathe.

"The legends give us signs to look for marking the end of all things. Not just Earth, but also our world beyond the Veil. Those signs are coming to pass. Among the final and most important signs is this infection that is trying to spread through the city. 'Creeping doom on tendrils of blue, like sky-sparks in miniature, the color of ice.' With other parts of the story we've pieced together, this infection matches all the clues. The story of the world given in the legend also matches current events. The end is coming unless we stop it. The Sword Society has kept the blade safe since before humanity rose to dominate the world and the Pures fled beyond the Veil, preparing for this day."

Bells nodded slowly, lips pursed. It did sound like the fungus, with its creepy electric-blue tendrils. Still... "Why me? I seem like a poor choice for this. I'm a farmer, and some other Pure would have an easier time traveling on some secret mission."

As Dawning opened his mouth, the elf responded first. "Because it must be you. The legends have many signs and Hawking has told us how they all match you."

Dawning said, "You and Jaekob, rather."

Bells did a double-take. "Jaekob? Both of us? That can't be."

The elf shrugged. "And yet it is. The legends speak of 'two Pure of heart and blood, one exalted by all, the other a mere servant.' When you showed up looking to meet the heir to the dragons, of all people, right before the infection began... Well, Hawking knows many more signs than I do, and he says it must mean you and Jaekob. The fact that the dragon is following you around tells us what we need to know. You met him ten years ago by chance, setting in motion all the events to led to *this day*, with you here when the outbreak began, accompanying the Dragon Prince." He flashed her a smirk.

Bells' jaw dropped, but she snapped it shut and her teeth clicked hard enough to hurt.

"Pure of heart and blood is a reference to you both being Pures—blood—but also pure of heart," Dawning continued. "Both of you are drawn to justice unless I'm mistaken."

"What do you mean? He's not fighting for my kind, at least not completely, so what kind of justice can he be drawn to?"

Dawning replied, "Jaekob did, after all, save you and your family from the troll and your foreman, kept you alive through extraordinary measures not often given a fae, and has followed you around ever since you arrived. You followed each other, rather. And you both were there at ground zero when the infection began. This cannot be a coincidence, and if you don't help us by fulfilling your destiny, both worlds die. But you do have a choice. You could sit back and die with everyone else."

Bells wanted to dismiss the tale as nothing more than the tricks of fairies or superstition, but something about the words he'd spoken in the legend made her heart skip a beat. And now, try as she might, she just couldn't bring herself to dismiss what they told her. It was like some ancient, primordial part of her recognized the words, like she'd heard them before, and now she had an itch inside her brain she couldn't scratch. That was the best way she could describe it.

"Why does it have to be both of us?" she asked.

Dawning smiled, though the elf and the were both frowned. Dawning said, "When the sword is needed, whether to unite or destroy the worlds, it protects itself. There are others who seek it, you know. Another group we've fought against since before the Egyptians first put chisel to stone to etch words. That group doesn't know this part of the legend, as we've kept it hidden through all this time."

The elf, still frowning, said, "The hidden part of the legend says this: 'Only the Pure but lowly can remove the sword from its tomb, but it is protected by a fire only a dragon can withstand, and neither spell nor glyph nor sleight of hand can change that fact.' Then, the legend says the lowly becomes the exalted. So you see, you two Pures must work together or you won't survive and get the sword."

That primordial part in Bells' brain surged as he told his story, and she felt like it was trying to scream inside her head that yes, she could do it, she was the one. But could she trust some vague sense? The world was facing a threat that could destroy it. She had felt that since the first time she saw the fungus.

She stood and looked at the other Pures. Her heart pounded in her chest like the rapping of a hungry woodpecker. Yet, she swallowed her fears. The plague would kill her family if she didn't go through with this. "Yes, I will go."

Her fear turned into excitement as an image came to mind, a picture of a cavern entrance.

Somehow, she knew where it was. The urge to leave was overwhelming. The cavern she'd never been to beckoned her to come to it.

"Now," Dawning said, smiling—no doubt he'd seen her aura shifting—"you have only to convince the dragon heir."

"I won't let you down," she replied, chin held high.

"Worry about the world, Bells, not us. Creation chose you for a reason. Remember that, when times grow darker before they get better."

Bells opened the door and blinked at the sunlight hitting her eyes. She was almost numb inside, like she'd been washed out. She tried to decide how she felt. "Empty" came to mind. And "determined," like a subconscious obsession was trying to break out and drive her toward the sword to rescue it.

None of the other fae inside had seemed to feel like they had to rescue the sword, despite knowing the legend long before she did. Perhaps she had a connection to the blade—something genetic, some hardwired instinct. Of all the Pures, the fae came closest to seeing the web that connected everything on Earth, so perhaps she was just getting a glimpse of the threads between herself and the sword, what some called fate. Fate was really just events navigating the web in the most likely way, not a predestination given by Creation.

She glanced at Jaekob, startled as she came out of her inner thoughts and saw the real world in front of her. "Jaekob?" she whispered as she tottered.

He rushed to grab her, then helped her sit on the front steps. "By Creation, you look terrible," he said. "Exhausted, and your eyes are bloodshot."

"I feel exhausted. Something happened in there—"

Jaekob reached for his spear, in its sling on his back.

Bells' eyes went wide. "No! I mean, I'm fine, but I'm wrung out. We have to go get that sword, Jaekob. They convinced me it's the only way to save not only Earth, but our world beyond the Veil, too."

"Lies," he said as he sat beside her. He glanced back to make sure the door was closed, his back not left vulnerable. "It's just an old legend some loonies have kept alive for thousands of years. It probably bears no trace of the original legend, in fact. They tend to shift over time."

Deep in her gut, Bells was certain that wasn't true. Not in this case. "When I heard the legend, or the part that applies to us—"

"Us?"

"Yes, us. When I heard it, I felt like a part of my mind came alive that I didn't even know was there. I *know* it's true."

"Sounds like an elf spell."

"No," Bells said, narrowing her eyes at him. "He cast no spells. I'd have felt it, I'd have seen his aura shift. The legend says a fae and a dragon will work together to bring the sword back, and together save the world. Not just any two, but us. You and me."

"And you believe this?" Jaekob stood and looked down at her. "It's nonsense. We need to go fight this infection before it spreads."

Bells stood, too, though still a bit wobbly, and gazed into his eyes without flinching. "No one can fight it, not without the power of this sword. And if only one of us goes, I'll fail and probably die. Both must go, or like I said, that fungus is going to destroy both worlds."

He stared back at her, standing motionless, but then he finally replied, "Tell me, then, how will a sword fight this fungus? You said it well when you said no one can fight it. Yet we're supposed to think a sword can fight it? That's silly."

Bells shook her head hard enough that a lock of hair came loose and got into her face. She tucked it over one ear as she said, "It doesn't fight the infection. Someone is making that fungus, and the sword will force them to stop making it. Only it can end the threat. What other options do we have? Or do you think you can just stab it with your spear, like any other enemy?"

He spun on his heels and flung his hand up toward her as he began to walk away. "It's a stupid legend, nothing more. I'm going to go do what we can in the *real* world to stop this infection from spreading. I won't let it destroy this world or any other."

Jaekob was wrong, and she felt it deep inside with the same certainty as she knew the ocean was blue and clouds were white. It was fundamental. "I'm going. If my dragon protector won't come, I may well die, but I'm not going to stand here marching in place with you while the world falls apart. I'm going to get that sword or die trying. Follow me to fulfill the legend or don't, but I'm leaving, whatever the cost."

She walked away and prayed she'd hear his footsteps rushing to catch up. Going alone would be her death, she was absolutely certain. But she would try, at least. Someone had to.

When she heard the scuff of sandals on the pavement, she allowed herself a faint smile. The Dragon Prince felt it too, just as she did. Of course he would come, and she'd happily let him think it was his choice, that he was going only to protect her. Whatever worked.

Bells opened her eyes with the dawning sun and stretched. For a second, she didn't realize where she was, only that the bed was the most comfortable thing she'd ever felt before. The sheets were wondrously smooth and soft. She smiled faintly and stayed in bed another few minutes, simply enjoying the feeling.

Her door opened and Jaekob stepped inside. She yanked the covers up to her neck, but Jaekob was polite enough not to comment about her sleep habits. Not polite enough to knock before coming in, though.

Bells glared at him. "Do you mind? I'm not even dressed. I'd prefer you knocked first."

Jaekob's mouth turned up impishly at the corners. "Oh, so sorry. It didn't occur to me to knock in my own house—and I saw much more of you when we were busy saving your life after the attack on my father."

She felt her face grow warm as her cheeks turned bright red. He'd seen *more* of her than this? She was mortified. Among the fae, modesty was held in high regard, but the dragons only wore clothing when they were aboveground. In the Warrens, she'd heard, they wore only a tool belt across their chests. Part of her wondered what he thought of his glimpses. She'd have been much less relaxed around him had she known. "That's humiliating. Why didn't you say anything before?"

He smirked at her and said, "It's not like I was concerned with your modesty. You were injured. Half your waist had been blown away and blood was everywhere. It wasn't pretty."

She let out a squeak and pulled the blanket over her head. "Argh, you're terrible. Can you please get out until I'm dressed?"

He closed the door behind him. Maybe he had only just realized a passerby seeing her in bed would embarrass her.

She peeked out from beneath the blanket. "What do you want? What couldn't wait until I'm up?"

He shrugged. "I just wanted to see if you were up. We have to leave on your ridiculous quest soon. But if you prefer, we can leave now and you can go in your current 'outfit.' I certainly won't mind." He grinned, and she nailed him in the face with her pillow. He made a great show of how much the pillow hurt, then beat a hasty retreat out the door.

Bells flew out of bed and reached for her clothes on the chair across the room, but looked twice in confusion. Those weren't her ragged clothes. Neatly folded on the chair, she saw a pair of human-made cotton pants—"jeans"—and a white cotton shirt of the sort humans called a "peasant's blouse." It had short, puffy sleeves but left both shoulders and her collar bare.

She had almost decided to refuse to wear it but then noticed there was also a rather pretty green coat and sturdy shoes with wool socks. At least with the coat, she could walk out of the room without dying of embarrassment from her bare shoulders.

When she left her room, she found Jaekob leaning against the wall in the hallway. He said, "Don't you look fancy."

She immediately felt her cheeks betray her again, blushing. He'd seen her in far less. "Thank you for the travel clothes, *Prince* Jaekob," she said, glaring at him.

He openly grinned at her, his eyes moving from her head to her toes and back again. "Well, you're fit for travel. Since we know where they hid the sword, I suggest we just fly there. We'll walk out of the city so no one sees me carrying you, then take off west. Unless you prefer to walk the whole way?"

Bells' eyes went wide and she covered her mouth. Dragons did *not* carry riders, especially not a mere fae, but he would let her ride him—a practical man. This wasn't at all what she expected from a dragon, much less the second most powerful person this side of the Veil. She remembered to nod after a moment. "It'll be faster," she said hesitantly.

"Good. Breakfast, then we leave." Jaekob led her to the kitchen, where Chef had piles of food waiting for them. When Chef saw her and Jaekob standing together, he smiled and his eyes sparkled. Bells didn't understand what was so amusing, so she simply thanked him and then sat to eat, trying not to look either man in the eyes.

Bells walked outside to meet Jaekob but stopped mid-step when she saw four dragons with him. His bodyguards, she recognized from before, and felt a flash of disappointment they were coming. "We'd make better time without them," she said, frowning.

Jaekob raised one eyebrow. "And you thought we'd just wander through the chaos? That's the world's worst date, if you ask me."

"It's not a date," Bells snapped. She took a deep breath. "I'm sure they'd rather stay home. Just because we have to go doesn't mean they do."

"They're coming. Mikah would have it no other way. Don't worry about it, okay?" Was that a wink he gave her? She watched his face for any hint at more but he turned away and started walking. "Time is wasting."

Bells followed. At first, she was lost in thought about how the guards would slow them down. The legend only said for the two of them to go, as well. Would bringing them ruin things? And was she really worried about their safety, or did she have a different worry, deep down? No, it was just the mission and their safety. She had to say it over and over again in her mind, not truly believing that.

Soon, however, the surroundings began to push her thoughts away, because as they approached the docks district, things became progressively more chaotic. Once, through buildings, she caught a glimpse of an entire squad of elf warlocks casting spells in unison at the Wards. Things must be desperate if the dragons were inviting elves to work on the Wards

She glanced at Jaekob, who had fallen into step beside her, and saw him clenching his jaw, his shoulders tense and hunched forward. Apparently, he didn't much care for the arrangement, but he looked far angrier than she had anticipated.

At the next glimpse down a street to their right, she saw the Wards again. Normally, they weren't actually visible without using magic-sight, but now the pulsating, sickly blue tendrils were actually growing *up the Wards* like ivy growing up a building. Already, the lowest six feet or so on the other side was only a solid mass of tendrils. Flashes of spells all along the Wards lit up the shell and the tendrils on the other side.

The streets were eerily empty on her side of the Wards, other than the elf and dragon casters reinforcing the city's only protection. Several casters were charred husks lying on the street, victims of the infection cleansed by magic and fire. She saw no elves wandering the shops, no fae shopkeepers shouting their wares from storefronts. Every door was closed, every window shade drawn, and many had boards over them as though the city was bracing for a hurricane. In a way, she supposed, it was.

In a low voice, she asked, "Why do you look so angry? Is it the elves working on the Wards?"

His lip curled into a snarl for just one moment, then he shook his head slowly. He didn't answer her, though.

She said, "All those poor Pures, hiding from the storm that's coming. It won't do them any good. Even the fae are hiding and they should know better." If the fae were frightened enough to disobey their foremen, things were already bad. Chaos would happen sooner than she had imagined possible.

"They aren't my concern," Jaekob said, glancing at her then away. "In the end, Mikah will have to order our retreat to the Warrens again to safeguard his own people and everyone else will get what they probably deserve."

"And yet here you are, coming with me to fight for them." She raised her eyebrows at him, confused.

He stopped mid-step, surprising Bells as she passed him by. She turned back as he said, "I'm not fighting for them. I'll never fight for them. It's not my fight, and none of these people are worthy of help."

"How can you say that?" Bells cried, using her hands to indicate the whole city. "These are Pures. Our people."

"Your people, not mine. I know what you're trying to do here, and I promise you, it won't work. The weres hunt innocent people, Pure and human alike, and they can pass from history for all I care. The trolls are mean, stupid brutes who only enjoy one thing—violence. The elves," his face suddenly turned to a snarl, "will be the first to die, if I have any say in the matter. So you see, they can all go to the abyss for all I care."

The anger in his voice startled her and she took a step back without realizing it. Her throat tightened, heart beating like a hummingbird as her eyes welled up, and she barely dared to whisper, "And what about the fae?"

He pursed his lips and let out a long, harsh sigh. "I told you before. You fae are all cowards. If you won't fight for yourselves, why should I? Now, come. We have a fool's errand to run, and I'm only here to make sure you don't get yourself killed—if I can, that is. We're walking into a trap, and you're about to get us both killed."

"Then why do you care what happens to me if the legend is just a stupid myth and I'm just a fae coward? Why not stay here if you're so afraid for your precious hide?" Bells couldn't believe she'd spoken to a Pure that way, much less *this* Pure. Her eyes grew round with surprise at herself.

Jaekob frowned, glaring at her. "I'm *only* doing this because you saved my father's life." He paused, then added, reluctantly, "And you had the guts to come to this city, saving your family with no foreman's note, no backup plan... You just left your village and came to fight the good fight. For a fae, you're as brave as a lion, and I respect that. But you're the only one I'd do this for, and you're the only fae who would ever do what you did, I suspect. You know how fae are."

Before she could snap an angry reply, he walked away, going fast enough that she had to jog to catch up. She didn't really want to walk with him after that, so she kept a couple paces behind him, silently fuming.

She played his last words through her mind over and over until Philadelphia's terrible condition pushed such personal thoughts aside. They passed the horrors on the other side of the Wards, and even one roped-off building on their side of the Wards that had tendrils creeping up the outer wall from the bottom floor. Bells was cautious not to touch anything just to be sure she didn't brush against a stray tendril; they had all seen the kind of death suffered by any who touched them.

A couple of hours later, they walked out of Philadelphia and into the woods north of the city, leaving the chaos and terror and horror behind, at last.

J.A. Culican

As Bells and Jaekob left the city, the mood became noticeably lighter. It was a beautiful day, and north of the city, the gently rolling, forested terrain brought back her connection with the plants and animals all around them. In the city, with all its pavement and plastics and buildings, she'd lost that sense of connection. She hadn't even realized it was gone until that moment, when the connections returned. It felt like a breath of fresh air after spending days in a dank and dusty basement. She couldn't help but smile.

Jaekob saw her smiling and the corners of his mouth ticked upward. "What has you in such a good mood?"

She flinched at the sudden interrogation until she saw his smile. It had been a reflex response and she cursed herself for not controlling it better. She replied, "It's just nice to be out of the city and back into nature. I know you're used to being surrounded by stone, down in the Warrens, but this is the kind of place we fae call home."

He nodded. Over his shoulder, he said to his Guardians, "This is far enough. You four, head back into the city and report in to assist with whatever the Dragon Council needs of you."

The one nearest Jaekob, the largest of the four Guardians, replied, "No, sir. We can't leave you out here. Our orders are to stand by you, whatever happens. We're here to protect you, sir."

Jaekob's smile faded a little. "I understand that. However, these are extraordinary circumstances. There is a legend, and it says that Bells and I must go ahead alone. I don't believe in legends, but since we're going to try every option, we're going to play by the legend's rules." His eyes narrowed and he added, "Now, go home."

The Guardians glanced at one another and then down at their feet, but didn't move.

Jaekob shook his head and from between gritted teeth, he said, "Listen, I know you're just trying to do your jobs. And I appreciate that. You've been brave and loyal, and my reports will reflect that. But make no mistake, you don't obey the Dragon Council—you and the Council all serve the First Councilor, and I speak with his voice. Get it?" Then he smiled, seeming to relax, and said, "Besides, when I rule in my father's place someday, I don't think you really want to be on my bad side."

He paused for a few seconds, waiting for a response, but none came so he continued. "I order you to report back to the Dragon Council. If you disobey me, you are disobeying my direct order in a time of crisis. You do know the penalty for that, do you not?"

Bells glanced back and forth between Jaekob and his Guardians. She had never seen dragons hold an open conversation like this in front of a mere fae, and she was particularly curious about the Guardians' reactions—they shifted from foot to foot, glancing anywhere but at Jaekob. Clearly, they were conflicted. And very nervous.

At last, one Guardian said, "Prince Jaekob, I hear and I obey." He went down on one knee, lowering his head and bringing his right fist over his heart, then turned and headed back toward Philadelphia. Then it was like a dam breaking as one after the other, the remaining Guardians followed his example.

In moments, the two were alone in the forest. "That was interesting," she said. "I don't think most fae have ever seen a discussion like that."

Jaekob shook his head. "Probably not. Maybe some of the house staff, but few others. Normally, dragons are very private. We handle our disagreements behind closed doors, away from prying eyes. Right now, however, we don't have the time for social niceties. We have to get moving, right?"

Bells nodded. She leaned against a tree with one hand, silently drawing strength and energy from not just the tree itself, but the things it touched: the beneficial bacteria and fungi in the soil around its roots, the ants and earthworms that crawled through it, loosening and enriching the soil, the roots of other plants and trees touched by the same mycorrhizae in the soil. In nature, everything was connected, and more than any of the other Pures, the fae were aware of their part in that web. They could draw upon it for strength.

She hoped Jaekob wouldn't notice what she was doing and tried to appear relaxed and casual. To distract him, she asked, "Now, how do we get to the cave? It will take us at least a week of walking. I told you this before we left and you said that was okay. I figure you must have some great plan to get around that."

He looked into her eyes, his face grave, and said, "I'm going to summon my dragon form, and you're going to ride on my back. We discussed this already." Something about the way he said it made the hairs on her arms stand up. There was more to it than the plain meaning of the words themselves.

Bells said, "Okay... I've never seen that done before, but you were right about time being short. It'll be scary, but I trust you not to let me fall."

Jaekob shook his head and then looked up at the tree canopy above, drawing a deep breath. He said, "Dragons never allow riders except in the gravest emergencies, and often not even then. But that infection is spreading fast, and I gave you my word that I'd follow this ridiculous plan of yours. I honor my word and will do what I can to help the plan succeed." He spoke slowly, his voice low and grave.

Bells thought she saw a hint of sadness in his eyes. Or was it worry? She couldn't quite peg what was going on. She stepped up beside him and put one hand lightly on his arm. "Are you sure about this? I get the feeling this is a very big deal for you, for some reason. I don't want to do anything that might hurt you, so if we have to walk, then the legends can just wait."

She forced a brave smile, or hoped it looked brave. It took real willpower to keep her eyes locked on his instead of looking away. Her curiosity was up, along with her concern for Jaekob, and she decided that his offer to carry her was the real reason he'd sent his Guardians away. She would have preferred they'd stayed with her if she and Jaekob walked into danger.

Jaekob nodded. "Thanks. I appreciate your concern, but no. As I said, I gave my word we would follow the old legend, at least until we rule it out."

Why had he even said he'd come with her? But he had indeed said he would come, and it didn't seem wise to ask about it just then. Clearly, he was nervous about something. He bit his lower lip and kept scratching his shoulder, his nostrils flared—a dragon's fear response? She had never seen that before.

She gathered her courage and said, "Okay, then. So, what's next? Do you turn into a dragon? And do I just climb on? That seems simple enough even for a fae to understand. Hopefully, I can hang on. Falling would be no fun. But like I said, I trust you."

Jaekob looked down at her, into her eyes, and she found herself bringing her hand up to her collar. Was she nervous? Blushing? She wasn't sure what made her suddenly so anxious.

He said, "When you first sit on me"—she tried not to laugh—"we're going to be vulnerable for at least an hour. I trusted my Guardians to defend us but I had to send them off. I don't want them knowing."

"Vulnerable? Why? And I thought they seemed pretty trustworthy."

"They are," he replied. "Still, they know what you're about to find out. The first time you sit on me, we're going to... Well, there'll be a connection between us, and that takes a while to sort itself out. It's why we'll be vulnerable. But in the end, we'll be able to speak clearly when we're together."

Bells frowned. "Connection? What does that mean, exactly? Like, I'll be able to ask you to turn left? That doesn't seem so horrible."

Jaekob took a step back. He put his hands on her shoulders and shrugged. "No, it's not horrible. But it is far more than that, as well. Rider and dragon form a sort of pair-bond. Not like handfasting, or whatever fae do when they marry, but also deeper. It's like a faint touch between souls so that we both experience everything the other does, at least when we're close to each other. I worry... I *wonder* what you'll think of that when you experience it. And I have things I prefer no one knew. I'm sure you do, too. Are you up for that? There will be no secrets between us once that bonding happens."

Bells froze like a deer in headlights, her mouth open in surprise as she experienced both thrill and terror at the same time. One coherent thought struck her: What if he didn't like what he saw in her head and ran, leaving her alone and far from home?

Bells found herself backing away from Jaekob, but after a couple paces, she forced herself to stop. There was much she didn't want this dragon—or anyone at all—knowing about her. And Jaekob was a famed warrior, born of a warrior people. The odds were good that he had things—memories and images inside of him—that she wanted no part of.

Worst of all, she had one thing in her head that she was only partly aware of, but she knew that she lied to herself about it. It was easy to pretend her way around that secret on the outside, but when they were connected, would he see the real truth? And would that mean she, too, had to face it head-on?

She coughed, her throat suddenly dry. Her voice came out raspy as she said, "Is there another way?"

He just shook his head. "Walking."

She closed her eyes and focused on getting her breathing back to normal and her heart to slow down. "I suppose that if I believe the legend enough to go look for the sword, I don't have much of a choice now that you've offered it. And if I don't believe it, then we shouldn't go at all. But I do believe. I'll do it, and thanks for offering."

"That's very wise of you, little fae. I promise that nothing I told you will compare to the actual bonding. Are you sure you want to do this?"

She suspected he wouldn't be disappointed if she said no, but they were trying to solve a problem that was bigger than either of them. Bigger than both of them together. "I'm sure," she replied.

An overwhelming feeling of both dread and anticipation flowed over her like a flash flood. She had to rest her hand on the tree again to steady her insides.

Jaekob pointed at her feet. "Stay there." He walked west until he was about fifty feet away, then he rolled his shoulders and neck, limbering up. "Here goes."

What Bells saw next amazed her as she witnessed, for the first time, someone summoning their dragon form. She heard snaps and crunching, as well as wet, tearing noises. For that instant of transformation, his face contorted into a mask of agony. But only for a moment, because the transformation was finished in only a couple of heartbeats.

Before her stood the dragon she remembered from that day ten years earlier, when Jaekob had spotted her from the air and dove down to talk to her—for no reason she ever knew. She doubted he had known why. It seemed obvious to her now that it was the legend that had spurred him to come down to talk to her—it had to happen that way, and so it did.

Jaekob, red scales shining in the dappled light that streamed through the tree canopy, had grown to fifty feet long from his snout to the tip of his tail. His head was as wide as his body, with massive jaws that she had no doubt could eat her in only two bites, if not in a single gulp. His tail curled around his feet, and his wings—the last to grow—spread out far to either side before he folded them back in on himself.

"Get ready, thennn sssit," he growled, and Bells felt the bass from his voice hitting her chest like a drum. It was awe-inspiring to see a dragon up close, even if it was the second time, and his aura, his voice, his presence—all were overwhelming. She found herself rooted to the spot. Her instincts told her to run, but she couldn't move at all. Her body refused to obey her, just as it had the first time he'd come to her.

A few seconds later, though, that feeling fell like a curtain on a stage, releasing her.

Jaekob growl-laughed—she remembered that sound, too—and said, "We havvve that effect on people, lllittle fae, during transssformations. Now, can we do this?"

Bells grinned, feeling sheepish. For whatever reason, that had been just about the most frightening thing she'd ever witnessed, even if the raw terror only lasted for a couple seconds. "Okay, here goes nothing," she said and strode up to the huge dragon.

She stepped onto his knee and up his thigh, using the wicked spikes growing in a row up his leg as handholds. Each spike was between two to four feet long. When she got to his massive hip, she reached up and grabbed one of the longer spikes growing along his back to pull herself up. Once on Jaekob's back, she crept forward toward his wings and then sat, straddling him with her legs hanging just forward of where his wings connected to his back. She wasn't quite on his neck, but close.

A moment after she sat on his back, a flash of light blinded her, and then there was only darkness.

J.A. Culican

Everything was pitch black. Not only that, but it was so quiet that Bells could almost hear the silence. She couldn't feel the solid scales and muscles of the dragon beneath her. Actually, she couldn't feel anything. She waved her hand—or at least, she thought she did, because she couldn't actually see it—and didn't feel the air moving, didn't feel her clothing shifting on her arm. Humans would have called it sensory deprivation, but Bells thought perhaps it might be the emptiness of death, and she felt a rising panic. Had Jaekob tricked her into a trap? Why?

Abruptly, she felt her first physical sensation, a swirling feeling in her head, like water swirling down a drain, but instead of water, her thoughts and memories flowed out of her skull. In the distance—far? Close? There was nothing by which to measure it—a pinpoint of light appeared. It rushed toward her, growing in size like the headlamp of an oncoming train. As she got closer to that light, she heard a faint sound, like a cacophony of voices all talking over each other.

And then the light slammed into her, too fast for her to even flinch. Suddenly, she wasn't in a senseless void of darkness.

Now she was in a stone tunnel, impossibly smooth like someone had used a torch to melt the stone surfaces. She heard someone talking, a woman, but only caught a fragment of it: "...and when the Germans are defeated, we'll go up to the surface and I'll show you what it's like to eat actual meat that you caught yourself, then..."

A cavern. Old, dusty. It looked utterly abandoned, though it contained dozens of decaying buildings. A sad feeling shot through her. The same woman from before said, "Of course. You're our pride and joy. You know that."

A plaza—no, not a plaza, but another cavern—this one so huge that she couldn't see the far side even with the odd glowing mushrooms on every wall. An angry man, scary and threatening, shouted, "Keep your spear up or I'll give you a nasty scar to remember the lesson, boy." The hulking brute stood several feet taller than Bells and swung a sword overhand at her head. She somehow blocked it with her spear without even thinking about it. And she blocked the next blow that came even harder. The one after that, however, drove her to her knees. "Here comes the pain, boy." Fire and pain across her left shoulder and chest. Blood. More pain.

Two huge people, a man and a woman, sat at a table with her. Though she couldn't see their faces, she knew these dragons were her father and mother. Love. Adoration. Her mother spooned goop onto her plate from a bowl. "Yes," her new mother said, "it's more gruel. All we could find were the little white mushrooms. Maybe tomorrow we'll find another kind. Now eat, so you can be big and strong like Fa." Disappointment.

A tunnel. A girl was there, a young woman, wearing only a bandoleer. The young woman smiled. "I found it," she cried. Part of the tunnel wall simply vanished. She smiled again and then ran into the new tunnel. Fear. Horror. No! Wait! Too late. An explosion engulfed the girl, and then death came for Bells, too...

Not death. Someone gently shook her awake. She wanted them to go away, to leave her to die. The girl was dead, she must be dead. Now, Bells would have to take over for her father. The life she had wanted as a blacksmith was gone, blown up with the woman. Bells' soul ached like nothing she'd ever felt before.

Another cavern. It had a pool. Elves! Hatred. Rage. Revenge. She drew her spear and charged the elves. Killed them. Another dragon her age but stronger—Bells didn't know how she knew that, but she was certain of it—was fighting the elves, too. One stabbed him and the scene froze in time. Every detail, crystal clear. Blood droplets. Horror. A rage that burned her soul from the inside. Loss. Pain.

Flying. Up a tunnel. Out of her home, into the great sky above. No walls! A thrill so powerful she felt giddy, even lightheaded. Into the sky, surrounded by thousands of others just like herself, dragons armed and armored for war. Adrenaline surged. War! It was beyond time for it. The elves would pay for what they did—whatever that was— once they stopped whichever human clan was engulfing the surface world in war. She hoped it wasn't the Germans again.

From high up, a dot on the ground far below. The dot was a person. It glowed, and she realized that this must be what it was like to see auras as the fae did. Poor fae—they never caught a break. But that was their problem. Her problem was the glowing dot below. She folded her wings and dove for a look, breaking formation. As Bells approached the ground below, she zoomed in on them. A fae... Her breath caught in her chest—so beautiful, that fae, but struggling. Bells felt protective of that little fae woman for some reason, in a way that was entirely new.

Then, guilt. What of Jewel? Well, it was no betrayal to her memory just to land and talk, was it? After all, the dragons needed to know what was going on in the world. No one would question that. Bells stretched her wings out and came to a teeth-jarring halt, then landed smoothly. Best landing ever! Did the fae notice? Why did she care if some fae girl noticed how smoothly she'd landed? But that face... Bells knew she'd never forget it, so beautiful and kind and open. But it was time to get back into formation. A quick conversation was all Bells had time for, so she rose into the air and forced herself not to look back. If she did, she might return to that fae. She couldn't get the woman's smile out of her mind, and she felt both fear and eagerness when she thought of seeing the fae again someday. If Creation had any justice, they would meet again.

More scenes, more feelings, a kaleidoscope of experiences continued to flood through her—

Bells blinked quickly as the vision faded like a mirage. She looked around, confused and stunned. She was on a dragon? Jaekob. Oh yes, she had mounted him to fly somewhere.

Her own memories flooded back, pushing out the visions like a fading dream. Those visions had mostly been hurtful, so she would prefer to forget them, but deep inside, she knew those had been Jaekob's memories. He must have experienced her memories the same way, gaining a lifetime in an instant.

She glanced into the sky and when she saw the sun, she gasped. It had moved far to the west. How long had she been in that vision state? So, it wasn't an instant, after all.

Two hours, Jaekob replied.

"Replied" wasn't right. His voice was bouncing inside her skull. His thoughts? Was that possible?

"Of course it's possible, little fae," he replied, though his mouth didn't move. He chuckled. *"Relax. I can't hear all your thoughts, nor you mine. You haven't learned to shield yours from me yet, that's all. It's just a matter of practice. You'll be able to do it without even having to think about it long before we arrive. I can't explain it, but where I grew up, mind-talk is normal. It was never as bright and clear as what I hear from you now, but I'm sure you can figure out why that is."*

She nodded. She had mounted him, and this was the reason his kind never bore riders—two hours in a trance, helpless, learning each other's secrets and experiencing them the way the person had. She tried to focus on the memories she'd experienced. Jaekob's memories. The visions had been so vivid, though, that she hadn't just witnessed them. She'd experienced them as though she had lived through many of his core life-defining experiences, feeling what he'd felt. Loved whom he'd loved. And so much more.

Tears came to her eyes. That poor dragon. She would have never guessed at the depths of feeling he possessed, whether in anger or love or simple curiosity. He may have shown the world a calm, unflappable prince on the outside, but inside, the man was a volcano of emotions.

There were uncharted depths in that calm pool.

"Er, you—" he started to growl, then stopped. He took a deep breath, then said, "No, I don't wannnt to talk abouuut it. I'm told it's just what happensss when sommmeone mounts a willing dragon. It'sss the curse of my people."

Bells shook her head. Curse? It was wondrous. Why, she wondered, had the dragons not made use of that fact long ago? "Jaekob, did you... see what I saw?" She frowned. "Did you see my life?"

She already knew the answer, so while part of her wanted to know what he thought of her life, the bigger part was humiliated. What must he think of her now that he'd seen what a frightened, broken person she truly was?

He didn't reply, just turned stared ahead of them. So, that would be a yes. He'd seen her life, too.

"It's not really a curse, you know. It's terrifying, yes, but it's also the most amazing thing I've ever seen. Dragon and rider each knowing what the other wants and needs, seeing what the other sees. That would be a heck of an advantage for your warriors, right?"

Bells caught a flash of an image in her mind, a picture of herself smiling. But it wasn't quite right; her faint childhood scar on one cheek was gone, as were the tiny lines around her eyes and lips. The Bells in that image was also bigger than she was, and she got a sense the girl in the image was brave and wild and loyal and happy; nothing like herself. She also caught a feeling, like a vague sense of longing, but it was confused and jumbled. And then it all stopped, like someone had closed the blinds to cover a window.

She sat in silence, shocked and confused. Beneath that, deep inside her, was also terror about what it all could mean. She was terrified but also thrilled in a way she'd never experienced before.

Realizing Jaekob might catch her thoughts as she had his, she shoved them away and tried to bury them. Foolish, stupid girl. She was a fae and he was a dragon—and they had a mission to get to. "Let's get out of here."

Jaekob launched himself into the air, wings beating powerfully. With every stroke, she felt his strong warrior muscles flex beneath her. Somehow, that majestic dragon got them up into the air and made it seem easy.

Her stomach lurched from the takeoff. Thrill and wonder filled her as they rode higher and higher. She heard herself laughing at the sheer joy of flying.

They flew fast—faster than Bells had ever thought possible—yet something about the magic of dragons kept their riders from being buffeted by the winds. She looked down at the patchwork quilt of land below but didn't see the landmark. "You sure you don't know what 'the Dragon's Teeth' are?"

I told you I don't. The closest thing I can think of is the Himalayas, but they're on the other side of this world. There are lots of dragon enclaves there, where we had to hold off the humans long ago, but we don't call it the Dragon's Teeth.

She frowned, but then an idea struck her. "You know, maybe it's not a dragon term. Maybe it's what the elves or fae call something. I never heard of it, so perhaps it's elven."

She felt a wave of embarrassment wash through her mind, courtesy of Jaekob's link to her. *I'm an idiot. Of course that's it. We've been trying to find what I'd call teeth, but that's the wrong perspective. Let me think.*

He banked left, then began a slow, lazy circle that spanned miles. Bells sighed and tried to wait patiently. Only a couple minutes later, however, he straightened out and headed west, accelerating.

"You figured something out?"

Maybe. There's an old elven myth about how they beat us in the first war between our kind—

"They did?" Bells was shocked.

No, of course not. But there was one battle they won, according to them. The elf king—they didn't have the Crown of Pures *back then, so each race had its own kings and queens—fought a battle they say they won.*

"But they didn't?" It seemed odd to her that elves and dragons had such different versions of the same event.

Not exactly. Their version is that their king fought our greatest champion and cut his fangs from his mouth. The fangs fell to the Earth and formed two mountains—the humans call them Mount Rainier and Mount Hood.

"That explains why we're streaking west. What's the dragons' version of the story?"

Both those mountains contained small dragon settlements. The elf barbarians tried to raid them with their human allies, slaves really, and used magic to blast into the mountains until they found a way in. The elves lost both battles, and the settlements survived until much later times, but a couple dragon warriors of renown did die in the fighting. The elves called those two the 'Fangs of the Dragons' back then, or so I learned from my mother.

Bells sat silently on his back as they flew onward, enjoying the feel of his mighty muscles flexing with each stroke of his wings. Dragons were indeed mighty beasts in their dragon form.

Thanks.

"Get out of my head, stalker. But seriously, don't you think an abandoned dragon settlement in remote mountains with few humans even today would be a great place to hide something?"

Yep. My money is on Mount Hood. Rainier is too volcanic and a huge section fell away during the earliest human civilizations, obliterating the Warrens there. Rainier was a military outpost. Hood, though, still has abandoned Warrens. It's dangerous, with lots of poisonous gasses that will kill any Pure besides dragons if they wander into a gas pocket, but it's intact.

"I'm not worried. You'll protect me. Wake me when we get there, I need a nap."

Jaekob chuckled in her mind and then went silent.

Soon after, she dozed off lying forward, her arms stretched to either side on his broad back and shoulders. Her last thought was the absurd idea that she was the first fae ever to hug a dragon.

Bells awoke with a start when Jaekob jolted her by landing. They were surrounded by snow, though the dragon magic that kept the wind from reaching her also kept her comfortably warm. She yawned, then grinned. "That was fast."

She looked around, then gasped at the breathtaking view from atop Mount Hood.

Yes, I sped up after you dozed off. But the effort of keeping the air calm around you kind of wore me out. You'll have to stay here for a bit while I go find something to eat.

"You can't just leave me here," she said, suddenly alarmed. "I'll die up here if anything happens to you."

No, if I'm not back in an hour, just head down the mountain. Not so hard, right?

She wasn't convinced. It wasn't as if she could fly down, and she didn't have winter clothes on. Speaking of cold, the wind was blowing fairly hard up there. She might freeze before he returned. She hadn't dealt with enough snow to know for sure.

Jaekob grunted. She realized he'd felt her concerns through their incredible link. But instead of arguing his point, he turned toward a boulder nestled up against a sheer facing and opened his mouth. A narrow stream of dragonfire struck the boulder and seemed to stick to it like burning oil. He kept pouring his breath onto the boulder until it faintly glowed. She could feel the heat radiating off it, even from ten feet away.

Stay close to that. You'll be warm long enough for me to get back.

Before Bells could reply, he launched into the air and, in a few beats of his mighty wings, he was gone.

She went to the sheer facing and sat down on a smaller rock. She didn't want to get muddy and wet, after all, and the boulder's heat was melting the snow all around it. She closed her eyes and waited.

Fifteen minutes later, Jaekob landed and the noise alerted her. She opened her eyes, then opened them even wider when she saw he carried a twitching cow in his talons. The next ten minutes were pretty gruesome as the dragon ate hundreds of pounds of beef, consuming everything but the thickest bones and its head.

He tossed the cow's head aside and it landed in the nearby snow, staring at Bells with vacant eyes. She covered her mouth and laughed at the strange sight, and Jaekob cocked his head to one side, his long neck curved into what almost looked like a question mark. That made her break out into a full belly-laugh.

He growled at her and she struggled to stop laughing. "I'm... sorry. It's just... that the cow head..."

He turned so his back was to her and Bells felt bad for hurting his feelings. She hadn't been laughing at him, after all. Well, except for the funny expression he'd made as a confused dragon.

There was a sound like paper tearing, and in seconds, Jaekob had summoned his human form. He had blood and bits of cow all over his face and he glared at her as he grabbed handfuls of snow to scrub clean. By the time he finished, he had regained his usual stoic expression. "If you're *quite* finished mocking me?"

She looked away, withering under his gaze. "I'm sorry, I wasn't laughing at you. Just, the way the cow head landed, it looked like the thing was staring at me while you ate the rest of it. It was funny. Morbid, but funny. And then you made, like, a question mark with your neck."

He hissed out a long breath. "Okay. I'm just not used to being laughed at, not by dragons and definitely not by—"

"By a mere fae?" she finished for him. She wasn't looking away anymore but staring him in his eyes.

"I was going to say 'by any other Pure.' I guess that's touchy for you."

"Yeah, I guess it is. Being a slave makes me a little touchy when my friends start looking down on me." She put her fists on her hips and faced him directly. "But I get that you're used to *everyone* being beneath you, not just me."

He started to reply, but she turned her back and started feeling around on the sheer mountain facing that formed the ledge's inner edge. "Where's the entrance?" she asked, trying not to sound angry.

Jaekob didn't speak, and Bells kept her back to him. After a few seconds, he broke the awkward silence. "Bells, I'm sorry. I didn't mean to offend you. Do you... Are we really friends, do you think?"

She froze in place and then slowly turned to face him. It was her turn to cock her head, confused, but her uncertainty was whether she'd assumed too much. She examined his face for any clue but saw only his usual flat expression. "I think we are. I mean, I'm just a fae, like you were going to say, so I don't expect you to wave at me in the market or take me to your favorite dragon tavern for dragon drinks with your dragon friends, but here, with no one else around to judge you? Sure, I think we're friends."

Before he could respond, she turned her back again and continued looking for an entrance. She didn't want him to see her hurt expression but was having a hard time hiding it. Maybe she'd gone too far. If he didn't leave her there to die, she would know he was more forgiving than most Pures. Even then, she'd be glad to have said what she said because it felt amazing to tell a Pure what she thought of him.

Jaekob surprised her, though, when he said, "That's not how we get in. I just needed to get some meat in my belly to get my energy up before we go in. There's a hidden doorway; I'll have to clear half the mountainside to find it. Before you ask, no, I've never been here. I know the entrance is here, but not exactly where because my mother had never been here."

Great. At least there were no more human armies in the region to take note of half the mountain snow vanishing in a cloud of steam. She wondered what he meant about his mother but let it go. She had higher priorities for the time being. "Should I get behind you when you clear it?"

Jaekob allowed a faint smile and said, "I would if I were you."

In minutes, Jaekob had melted half the snow on the mountain. There hadn't been much of it this time of year, but certainly enough to hide a doorway. Once the steam cleared, Bells stepped out from behind him and saw the portal. It was a massive archway, easily large enough to allow two dragons in beast form to pass through side by side. The outer edge had runes carved into it, but they weren't ones she recognized. They were mostly lines and V-shapes, and they glowed faintly.

"How did the humans never find this?" she asked. "It's huge, it glows, and it obviously isn't natural. They're curious things, the humans. Or so I'm told."

"Easy," he replied, "only those with a connection to Creation can see the runes. Humans lost that connection long before they could have found this place. It just looks like an impassable rocky outcropping to them."

"How do you open it?"

Jaekob frowned. "How in Creation's tears should I know? I figured they told you that when they explained the job to you."

Bells shook her head. "Nope. I just figured you'd know. Dragon place... Dragon runes..."

He shrugged, lips pressed tightly together. He stepped up to the grand arch and the runes grew brighter. He touched the nearest one. "Elomite, I think. It's pre-history Persian, basically. One of the very first written languages. I may be able to sound it out."

As he experimented with different words Bells didn't know, she stepped up to the still-warm boulder and waited. After almost half an hour, though, they still hadn't made progress. Bells walked up to the entryway. "Jaekob, we'll never get in at this rate. But you just ate and recharged, right? So maybe you could, I dunno, melt it? Burn through it."

"Maybe. Dragonfire is hotter than just about anything on Earth, certainly hotter than what elves can create with their magic. Maybe the builders never expected a dragon to try to force his way in, and if that's the case, they may not have warded the stone against that."

Bells smirked. "Great. Less talking, more melting."

He chuckled and stepped a bit closer, motioned her behind him, then began what Bells could only have described as a furious, hellish assault on the stone archway doors. In minutes, the stone doors melted down to thick lava, the red glow fading to black.

Without looking at her, he said, "I suspect you can't get past this. It'll be hot enough to melt your face for hours."

"Well, then, with your permission, I'd appreciate it if you'd summon your beast form and carry me through the doorway. If you can protect me from freezing, suffocating, and being blown away while you fly like a meteor, I'm sure you can take a little heat. You can handle the heat, can't you?" She grinned, feeling mischievous. Let him figure out what she meant by that look, hah.

He paused only long enough for Bells to tell she'd had the desired effect, then he summoned his dragon form. They passed through the doorway and landed on the far side, and he summoned his human form again. Bells looked around in awe. She was in an ancient place, a dragon place. It was a place of legend, and it might well hold a sword out of myths and legends.

How could a simple fae have gotten herself into such a mess? Her kind simply did not go on such adventures. She wondered what her dear parents and siblings would think of what she was doing. She couldn't wait to find out.

"It's beautiful," she said aloud to herself. And it was. Glowing mushrooms grew evenly, even after this part of the Warrens had been abandoned several thousand years ago. The floor, walls, and ceiling were all glass-smooth, and the dragons had given the floor traction by melting elegant patterns and designs into it. Elegant, but stark and simple, like dragons themselves, she mused.

Jaekob replied, "Thank you. Most Pures hate our Warrens, but they don't see the art that goes into every foot of it. You can see the glowshrooms in here?"

It was pitch black inside the mountain, but she realized with a sudden surprise that yes, she could see at least a couple hundred yards; glowing mushrooms cast faint light that far. "Yeah. How did that happen? Are the mushrooms enchanted to let Pures see in the dark here?"

He shook his head. "Nope. In fact, I'm not sure how you could come inside at all. The Wards are still up and were strengthened after the elf surprise attack." He paused and looked at her curiously, cocking his head.

"What?" She shrunk under his intense stare.

He shrugged. "It must be because you rode me. The bonding has never been done to another Pure race, not that I ever heard, anyway. There are legends of humans who once rode some of us, in the days of ancient Egypt and before, but the same legends say we stopped that when they began to develop writing. We didn't want everyone to know it was possible, so we stopped altogether."

"Maybe it is from riding you," she said, raising her eyebrows. "If the Wards are up and I can see in pitch black instead of needing at least the moon's faint light, then that has to be the reason. Well, let's take advantage of it and go find this sword."

"Your sword. I'm not fighting, I told you that. If you want to fight, you'll need it more than me. Come on." He walked on.

Bells kept pace beside him in the entry tunnel until it led into a vast chamber so wide that, despite the glowing mushrooms, she couldn't see all the way across it. Many other tunnels led from the chamber, even in just the part she could see.

Jaekob said, "Wow. Does the legend they tricked you with say which tunnel to take?" He chuckled, but it sounded forced. He must have been trying to keep a positive attitude.

"Nope. Let's walk around the edge and see if any of the tunnels have signs. 'Ancient sword this way, two-hundred meters,' or something."

He smiled and motioned for her to lead the way. They followed the wall left from the entry, pausing at each new tunnel to look for any indication as to which way they should go. Some tunnels were small, only large enough for a single transformed dragon to pass through, but most were wide enough for two. They stopped when they got to one that was large enough for four dragons abreast.

"This tunnel looks important," Jaekob said. "I think an important sword might be down an important tunnel."

Bells paused. She reached out with her senses, going as far as she could, but felt nothing unusual. Just the living mountain itself, and glowing fungi. "Let's at least check the other tunnels first, and then we can come back."

They passed more tunnels. One appeared half-collapsed, and Jaekob spent long minutes examining the archway runes, maybe trying to decipher them in his head for clues, but at last, he shook his head. "I don't think it's this way. They wouldn't have left it in an unstable segment in case it collapsed more over time."

That made sense so she continued onward. After half a dozen more openings, they were about three-quarters of the way around the monstrous cavern and she could no longer see the entry tunnel when they found another collapsed one. Actually, she realized, it was really just a crevasse. Jaekob didn't even slow down, so she followed him. His reasoning had been good the last time they'd found a collapsed tunnel, and nothing had changed.

Until Bells felt—something. She stopped mid-step, freezing by reflex as her mind tried to catch up to what she'd felt. "Wait..."

Jaekob stopped and turned back to her. "Come on, slowpoke. If we don't find a clue by the time we get back to the entrance, we'll start wandering the tunnels. Dragons never get lost underground, so don't worry about that."

He started to walk onward, but she stayed frozen, closing her eyes to focus on her sixth sense. She sent it out as far as she could, down that crevasse-tunnel, and she felt the *something* once again.

Actually, it wasn't so much that she felt something down there. It was more like the *absence* of something. It was like she sensed a void, a nothingness.

"What is it?" Jaekob asked from right beside her, but she didn't open her eyes. She fought to locate the void's source, focusing on it with all her will. Her forehead grew damp from the effort. And then she sensed it again, this time longer and stronger. It definitely came from somewhere down the collapsed tunnel. The void didn't feel wrong, not like something that shouldn't be there. Whatever it was, it belonged there, but the idea confused her. Everything had a place in the order of things, but not this void. Wherever this thing was, it *owned* its space. The image of a king on a throne flashed through her head.

She smiled. "It's down this one."

"That's just a collapsed tunnel," he said, stating the obvious.

"No, it isn't. There's something down there, something strong. It's absorbing my senses when I cast them that way, no matter how hard I focus on it. And though I'm not a dark-dweller fae, like some in Asia, I don't feel like this stone is damaged. I think it's just a crevasse, not a collapsed tunnel. Or they only made an entryway to the crevasse and the new entry collapsed but the crack beyond it is fine. It goes on farther than I can cast my senses."

He frowned, looking confused. His aura was tinged with brown, confirming he was.

"What's got you baffled?" she asked. He might well have known things she didn't, and she decided it would be best to find out *before* she charged down a long crack in the heart of a volcanic mountain.

"I was just trying to see if what you said made any sense, and well, there are no glyphs and symbols around this one. No markings of any kind. Why would they do that?" He paused, then grinned and snapped his fingers. "That must be where the soul pool is."

"The what?"

Jaekob pursed his lips and paused, and she sensed his aura outlined in faint yellow. He must feel fear, or maybe doubt. She fought the urge to ask more questions, instead waiting for him to decide on whatever hesitation had given him conflicting feelings.

He closed his eyes and let out a long breath. "Well, there's no harm in telling you, I suppose, but don't go spreading it around. It's an open secret that dragon settlements each have a soul pool. Safeholme has the largest one in this world, of course. Soul pools are where our spirits go when we die, always to the nearest one. Our souls fly to the pool and merge with it. The energy from those souls is what gives dragons all our powers, including summoning our dragon forms, runecasting, the Wards, and our ancestor artifacts."

Bells stared at him wide-eyed. Soul pools? Ancestor artifacts? Runecasting? "So, what happens to the souls that get used to power up your mojo?"

He smiled at her and patted her head gently as if she were an amusing child. She glowered at him. That only made him smile more. He replied,

"Nothing happens to the souls. Their power is endless, the only limit being what we can do with that energy and how fast. More souls, faster use by more dragons."

Actually, she realized, it wasn't much different than what happened to fae when they died. Fae believed their souls got absorbed by the living world around them. It was the living world that gave fae their powers, just like the soul pools for dragons. The Earth might be just one big soul pool, but for fae.

"Then," Jacob continued, "when an egg reaches a certain point in development, a soul leaves the pool to merge with the dragon inside the egg. That's when they begin to commune with their mother and absorb her knowledge, skills, and memories. Why, when do fae do that?"

"Do what?" It was her turn to feel confused.

"Commune with your mothers? Absorb what you'll need to survive and thrive after you hatch. I mean, after you're born."

Bells stared at him, dumbfounded. After the long pause started to feel awkward, she broke eye contact with him and figured she should say something in reply. "Sorry. I don't mean to stare. We don't commune with our mothers. None of the Pures do. Well, except for you, I guess. I didn't even know that was a thing."

His mouth opened in surprise. Then he said, "So... How do you learn what you need to survive when you're born?"

"We don't, silly. Our mothers take care of us until we can walk and talk—"

"—Just like dragons do."

"Yeah, but the difference is that we learn what we need by learning it. We study, we teach each other, we practice. We hear the trees whispering to us the history of our clan. The grass tells us about the fungi and insects and worms, the life below the surface. The crops tell us how to water them, what to put into the soil for them, how to harvest them, and how many seeds to set aside. We memorize it, but it's all after we're born."

"You can't talk when you're born?"

"Can you?"

Jaekob nodded. "Yeah. This is interesting, but let's talk about that later. What's down this simple crack?"

She gave him a lopsided smile. "There's only one way to find out."

He shrugged and squeezed into the crevasse, and she followed. Together, they wiggled their way forward, yard after yard. When they got to the last glowshroom they could see—which Jaekob seemed to think was odd because they usually grew naturally throughout a cavern system, never growing close to another one but filling every available space down here—he pulled his knife out and sliced the mushroom from the wall. "Into the unknown," he said, handing the glowing fungus to her as she took the lead.

Long after they passed beyond the reach of the final glowshroom on the wall far behind them, holding up the one Jaekob had cut off for her, Bells said, "See anything?"

"You're in front."

"Yeah, but all I see is rock. It can't be in a place like this, can it?"

"I don't know, but this was your idea if I remember—" Jaekob started, but before he could finish, they emerged into a rough, natural-looking cavern complete with stalagmite columns. "Didn't you sense this chamber? You could have warned a guy."

"No, I didn't. It just felt like the crack kept going. What does that mean?"

He furrowed his brow, staring ahead blankly, but then looked back at her. "I think it means this is entirely natural. You only sensed the crack in the wall because of the glowshrooms, right? After that, we had to rely entirely on what we could see with our eyes?"

"Yes. I guess that makes sense. Maybe this cavern was the void I sensed."

Jaekob shook his head. "I doubt it. After all, you didn't sense a void in the crevasse at any point, and we went through maybe half a mile of it."

Bells tossed the glowshroom into the cavern's center, lighting up the entire room. It was small compared to the one they arrived in, no more than fifty feet across. Four columns were evenly spaced around the cavern, the upper stalactites and lower stalagmites having grown together long ago. Otherwise, the cavern was entirely empty. It was also humid, and she realized as she wiped her brow that it was horribly hot.

Jaekob seemed not to notice the heat, though, and walked around examining the walls, ceiling, and floor, looking calm and cool.

"Aren't you hot?" she asked.

"Nope. Heat doesn't bother us, you know, but if it bothers you too much, just take off some layers of clothes. And it's hot here because we're in the heart of a volcano."

"I'm good." She had known it was a volcano, but she hadn't expected to be so close to the magma. Or maybe there were lots of cracks like this one throughout the mountain, some full of magma rising. It was an unsettling thought. "So, where's this sword? It's supposed to be here. I know it is."

"Maybe, but I don't see it. No altar, no display case, nothing. I don't sense any illusion hiding it, either."

Bells closed her eyes and focused on feeling the unique vibrations that enchanted items created but found none. "I don't know. Maybe more light would help." She walked up to the glowshroom on the floor and over it, she began weaving a simple pattern in the air over and over again. The pattern glowed faintly at first but brighter with each pass of her hands. She muttered under her breath, but as the light grew brighter, her voice rose louder.

When she stopped chanting, she thrust her hands out to her sides, palms facing upward. The glowing glyph hung in the air and then drifted down onto the glowshroom, merging with it. The room was suddenly bathed in bright light—not just a glowshroom's weird glow but real light, as bright as day. Bells smiled at Jaekob, but he stood motionless, tense, eyes narrowed and locked onto something. She followed his gaze—and froze. In the light, the four natural columns were semi-translucent. Within one was the unmistakable shape of a sword.

"No flipping way," Jaekob muttered. She couldn't have agreed more. "Do you see what I see?"

"Yeah," she said and walked up to the column. "How'd they get it inside this stalagmite? Or is it a stalactite?"

"When they grow together like this, they're called columns. And I have no idea. Maybe they stuck it into a stalagmite and the column grew around it. I'm not sure how long that would take, though."

"I guess it doesn't really matter. So, what do we do? Shatter the column?"

Jaekob walked around the column, touching it with his fingertips lightly. "That would be a shame, but it might be required. I would never have found this without you—not that I'd even be looking for it if it weren't for you."

"I can't believe it's this simple. I guess you're right, we're going to have to smash the column to get it out." She stepped away from the column to give him room. "Hulk, smash."

He grunted and pulled his spear from its sheath. He held the tip to the side of the column and stepped back, gripping his spear like a baseball bat. "One. Two. Three—" He swung his spear hard, the tip making a whistling noise through the air, and it smashed into the column.

Shards of stone flew in every direction as it came apart in a dozen big chunks, and the sword clattered to the stone floor, its metallic ringing echoing off the walls.

Jaekob whistled. "Oh, wow. Look at that thing. It's beautiful."

Bells looked down at it, hesitant to touch it. It didn't look like much for such a mythological weapon. How disappointing... "What's so special about this?" she asked.

"Everything. I mean, look at the shape. It's a scimitar all right, but not like any I've seen. And see the grain in the guard? It's not Damascus steel, as the humans call it, but it sort of looks like it. More like the grain of wood from a tree, really. And the whole thing is roughly made, like something crafted far before its time. Look at how beautiful the grip is. That's got to be ironwood. Maybe African? It doesn't look like Persian ironwood, and none of the species from North and South America were available when they forged this thing. I guess it could have been available—dragons can fly around the world, of course—but I doubt it. No one knew of the Americas at that time according to the records."

"Does it matter where the wood is from?" Bells scratched her head.

"Not really, except that it's a beautiful weapon. I just appreciate what it took to forge this sword back then. It doesn't look nearly as polished as the blades we make now, but—hey! Look at that, there are glyphs etched into the blade along the spine."

Bells gasped. "They're glowing a little."

He moved to look at it from different angles. "You're right. I don't even know how powerful those must be to glow now, outside of battle. That's incredible."

Bells looked more carefully and saw the sword had a weird, mottled look along the spine, the side opposite to the cutting edge. "What's that splotching? I don't even have a word for what that looks like."

He nodded, his eyes lighting up faint red. "I do. 'Morbilliform.' That's what molten metal looks like when hammer-welded onto another piece of metal. It can even be done with two different kinds of metal altogether. It's beautiful, even if the effect gives people a vaguely creepy feeling."

She didn't think the "morbilliform" was beautiful. The sword looked crude, like some kind of fire demon had dripped sweat onto the weapon while forging it—though she, unlike her father, knew very little about blacksmithing. Or demons. To be polite, she nodded.

"Well," he said, "you wanted it and now you have it. Grab that thing and we'll be on our way."

She hesitated. "You're a warrior. I've never trained for battle. I think it'll do more good in your hands."

He shook his head, jaw clenched. "No. First, it was a group of other Pures who told you about this thing and I don't trust them. Second, I told you I'm not fighting. This world deserves what it gets as far as I'm concerned. You want to fight? Then you do it."

"I thought you'd changed your mind," Bells replied. What a waste. He was one of the best warriors in both worlds. What could make a man like him become so jaded? But she'd seen many of his memories when they linked and it made a certain kind of sense. He'd lost so much due to others fighting and now he tried very hard not to care. It was more likely that he used not caring as an armor to protect himself from getting hurt again.

He made no move to pick up the sword.

Fine, someone had to take it if they were going to save the Earth. Maybe even save the other side of the Veil, for that matter. She bent down and grabbed the scimitar by its hilt. "So this is *Shmsharatsh*, huh?" She turned it over, examining the construction. It seemed crude but effective, not nearly as polished as the swords her village forged. "I thought something earth-shaking would happen when I picked up the mighty Sword of Fire."

"Apparently not. Let's get out of here and try to make it home before dinner." He smiled and walked with her toward the crack in the wall that would take them back to the main chamber and then up to fresh mountain air.

The hairs on her neck stood and she paused, startled. Something felt wrong. She thought about it for a moment and finally it came to her. "Is it hotter in here than when we came in?"

"I don't think so. But then again, I'm not the best one to—" He paused, too. "Did you feel that? Like the ground moving? Not shaking, exactly. More like... I don't know, vibrating."

She shook her head, but both of them turned to the columns when their glowshroom-powered light shifted from a sort of yellow-brown into a reddish color. Beads of sweat formed on her neck and forehead, and the chamber was hot enough to make her feel lightheaded. "I think we should get out of here," she said, already moving toward the crack.

They didn't waste time talking—the temperature still kept rising. It was becoming hard to even breathe, the air was so hot. Then she smelled something odd, like fermented eggs, and her eyes and lungs began to sting.

Her leg buckled and she went to one knee. She saw Jaekob bending over her but couldn't make out his words. Ignoring him, she tried to get up again to keep moving, but her vision grew dim and panic washed over her. Suddenly, the ground rushed up at her—

She blinked rapidly, the wind bitingly cold. She was lying on something cold and wet. She tried to move but her body just wouldn't obey. Snow, she realized. She was lying on snow. What in Creation had happened?

Jaekob! Where was he? She moved her head to look around, frantic, but found him kneeling beside her. She became aware that he was holding her hand. His eyes were closed and his mouth was moving, but all she heard was a bird-of-prey cry far above them, and a deep rumble from below. The mountain was shaking. She sat bolt upright, but he put one hand on her chest and pushed her back down.

This time, when he spoke, she heard his words. "Stay down a moment, I'm not done yet." He went back to muttering something.

The biting pain in her eyes and lungs faded and her vision, which had been narrow to the point where she could only see a bubble of light in the middle of a black cloud, widened slowly until the black frame around her field of vision disappeared.

He let go of her hand and slumped, head dropping.

"Jaekob, are you all right? What's going on?" She scrambled to her feet and wrapped herself around him from behind. "Jaekob?"

He didn't answer, staying motionless on his hands and knees with his head hanging down. At least he was alive, though.

She stood and looked around, trying to get her bearings. The sight of lava moving slowly through the entryway startled her. It flowed out through the arch and slowly downhill. She and Jaekob were about one hundred feet away, far enough that she could just feel the heat on her face and arms. Noxious smoke billowed out the entry and up into the sky, seeming to go up for miles.

The volcano had erupted. Dragons were immune to all but the most extreme heat, could hold their breath for many minutes, and could breathe air that would kill other Pures. It was a side effect of living underground since the dawn of history, but Jaekob had obviously reached the extent of his abilities.

"I need water," he croaked. She gathered snow into her hands, already slushy from the heat when she gathered it, and let it finish melting. Then, she poured a little from her hands into his mouth. When the little swallow of water was gone, she got more.

After she'd done that three times, he smiled and held up one hand. "Thanks. I'm okay, now."

She wrapped her arms around him again and buried her face in his neck. "Thank you, you idiot. You saved me, didn't you? Instead of just running, you carried me out. Why?"

"You needed help," he said with a raspy, dry voice.

Everyone needed his help, but he'd helped her alone. She grinned, face still in his neck and shoulder. "Thanks."

He took a ragged breath. "If you hadn't noticed the heat first, I wouldn't have known until I smelled the gas. We made it out with only seconds to spare. I think we saved each other."

She helped him to his feet, then grabbed the sword from where it lay in the snow and handed it to him. He shook his head, hands held out. She said,

"I don't have anything here to strap it to me, and when you summon your dragon, it'll transform with you, right? Let's not drop it over Montana, shall we?"

He huffed but took the sword and strapped the sheath to his belt. "Okay. Whoever said we should get out of here if we're going to be back in time for dinner was right. I'll be so hungry I could eat a horse."

Bells laughed to discover it wasn't just a human figure of speech. She just hoped he didn't eat the horse at the dinner table. A dragon devouring a big animal was a pretty wicked sight.

As Jaekob finished his third barrel roll, Bells closed her eyes and enjoyed the feel of the light breeze. She had asked him to allow a bit to reach her as they flew. She'd been nervous to fly the first time, but to her surprise, she discovered it was a crazy rush and insanely fun.

As her stomach settled, she looked up into the night sky and gazed at the bright, full moon and the twinkling stars above; they looked amazingly close and crystal clear from this height. She felt Jaekob shifting speed and banking a little to their left and looked around. Below, she spotted a herd of elk or deer. Her mount must be hungry by now, she realized.

I am, Jaekob's voice echoed in her head. *Just a quick bite and then we'll get back to Philadelphia.*

"Okay," she replied. "I can't ask you to fly into the city hungry. We don't know what we'll find." She frowned as thoughts of their problems came back, replacing the thrill of flying, barrel rolls, and the moon and stars above. "I wouldn't ask you to walk into that without being at top strength."

Jaekob banked harder as they spiraled downward. She grabbed onto him as tightly as she could just before he pounced on an elk with big horns. It was no match for a dragon, though, and barely had time to shriek before it died. The other elks fled as Jaekob began tearing hunks of meat from his prey.

Bells decided to stretch her legs for a bit and slid off his back. She hung off one wing where it connected to his back and then dropped to the ground. She walked away toward nearby trees as she put her hands on the small of her back, leaning backward to stretch. When she got about ten feet from Jaekob, though, her connection to him vanished. When she'd gone another few feet, her senses reached the tree line itself. Suddenly, she felt something else—raw seething anger and an insatiable hunger. The sensation struck her like a hammer, stopping her in her tracks. She somehow knew those feelings were being directed at *her*. Some sort of sixth sense made a shiver run up her spine.

She focused harder, looking more carefully to identify the possible threat. She felt a dozen creatures in the tree line. Not people, not animals, but something *in between*. She could practically taste their magic on the back of her tongue as she breathed. She'd felt that before, she realized. They were werewolves on the hunt.

Her hands shook with adrenaline. Desperately, she tried to back up toward Jaekob but her body wouldn't obey. She was so terrified that she couldn't move, couldn't scream. She could only stare at the tree line as a dozen dark shapes came shooting from the trees in a V-formation. They were moving so *fast*, loping along on two legs, standing upright.

They had impossibly long arms and used them to run even faster, like gorillas. They were even bulky like gorillas, but they were definitely wolf-like. Their eyes glowed red, and all dozen pairs stayed locked onto her.

Run, dammit! She couldn't move. All she could do was pray to Creation that Jaekob saw them before they ripped her limb from limb. She had no doubt they were coming to devour her but she had a sense they were looking for something else, too. Perhaps they recognized Jaekob, even in his dragon form.

A blur of movement blew by her on the right and came to a stop six feet in front of her. It was Jaekob in his human form and he was poised to strike with the new sword in his right hand. It glowed brightly in the darkness from the runes etched into the blade, flickering between yellow, orange, and red.

For just a second, Bells stared in awe at Jaekob, crouched and ready for battle, the scimitar he'd carried during flight now held over his head with its point toward the oncoming werewolves. He cut a striking figure, reminding her of a hero in the old tales or human storybooks. He stumbled and she got the distinct impression the sword had been frozen in place for a split second, but once he recovered his footing, the blade seemed to move just fine in his expert warrior's hands.

The first werewolf leaped through the air at him, but Jaekob made the sword dance as he dodged the attack, the werewolf landing behind him. In that instant, the were had three new, deep cuts on his leg, arm, and side.

For a moment, everyone froze and looked at the wounded were, surprised. The cuts... They glowed, and Bells would have sworn she saw sparkles along the edges of the parted flesh. The sparkles increased, more and more of them flashing brighter still. The smell of burned meat hit Bells' nose. The wounded were threw his head back and howled the most agonized, sad, frightened sound Bells ever heard. As his howl went on and on, the sparkles spread outward from the cut, burning fur and flesh, and seconds later, they consumed the were from the inside. All that remained was a statue of glowing-hot ashes that broke apart and scattered in the wind.

Jaekob was the first to break through the total shock and surprise. He held the sword with both hands, sweat trickling down his forehead. His voice was heavy with exertion, roaring at the weres, "Hold or die. Harm her and I will hunt you to the ends of the Earth and beyond."

One of the weres, a huge male with black fur, stood upright. He shifted to his human form in only seconds. It looked terribly painful the way his six-inch claws retracted into his hands, arms shrinking with a wet, crunching noise, muzzle drawing back and changing shape amid crackling bones, until he was just a man again. The other weres then did the same as the black-furred man knelt in front of Jaekob and bowed his head.

"You have slain the pack leader, Dragon Prince. By the law of the pack, I am now our leader, but you have earned more than your lives. We swear our loyalty to you, Jaekob son of Mikah, and as long as you live, we will not leave your side. This I swear by Creation's will."

The others knelt, too, and Jaekob straightened up from his combat crouch, wary and confused.

Bells felt something in the air but couldn't put her finger on it. Something magical. Something of the *old* magic, powerful but wild.

Jaekob backed up to where she stood, never taking his eyes off the weres or lowering the ancient sword, and whispered, "Something isn't right."

"I know. I feel it, too."

"No," he said, shaking his head, "not that. The sword. It... It's like it is resisting me. It doesn't want me to move it, and it would have been happy if I'd died fighting the weres. I don't know why or how, but this is more than just some magic sword."

The lead were stood and the others rose with him. "My lord, we are yours to command."

"Fine!" Jaekob shouted. "If you won't leave me, then you can try to keep up. I'm going back to Philadelphia and I'll be flying. Leave us now and see if you can make it there alive."

The were bowed, turned, and ran east. The remaining ten weres ran after him, forming a single line and overtaking the pack leader until he was in the rear, where he could see his whole pack.

"Just like real wolves," Bells muttered.

Jaekob looked over at her, startled. "Yes. Very observant. Few people ever see a pack and live. But they are real wolves, you know. Half wolf, anyway. I don't think they'll make it to Philadelphia alive. They'll either run off into the woods again or get killed by the terrible things said to now wander the wilderness."

"What terrible things?" Bells had heard no such rumors.

"In lands where neither Pure nor human live, there are things coming to this world through the rift created by the Veil. Things not from our lands beyond the Veil, whatever they are. We find only skeletons, picked clean even when we come to rescue them only an hour later. We don't know who or what is eating the Pures, but thank Creation there aren't many. Not yet."

Bells shrugged. As scary as that sounded, she wouldn't have to deal with them when she traveled by dragon. "Did you see the wounds that sword made? There was no chance to even clean them up. I wonder if even a scratch would kill someone."

He frowned, which was not at all the reaction she expected from a warrior with a new and deadly weapon. His voice dropped low almost to a whisper despite being alone with her, and he said, "There's something wrong with this sword. It scares me. I'm telling you, this is not the answer we need for our problems. I don't think you should take it to the city, or anywhere else. We should have dumped it into the lava at Mount Hood. It's not too late—"

"No!" she cried. "The infection is spreading, and the world could die. The whole world, Jaekob. Not just the humans you abandoned to the Pures, but all of us. The only people with any idea how to stop the infection said we need this sword. Until you have a better idea, don't toss it away. Please! I don't want my little sister to die from that fungus the way your Guardian did. It's too horrible to even think about."

He paused, but then nodded and looked away.

Bells said, "Truly, thank you. We should hurry, though. We're running out of time. Are you fed?"

Jaekob nodded but he didn't smile the way he had the last time he hunted with her. She didn't blame him; despite what she said to him, the truth was that the sword had given her a strange and unsettling feeling, too, when the runes glowed as it was pulled in battle. There was more to the sword than they knew.

Bells poked the small fire, lost in thought. Jaekob had insisted on stopping to rest, so they'd taken shelter in an abandoned parking garage along an old human highway. It was exhausting, he said, trying not to throw the sword away mid-flight, and he didn't want to return to the city weakened in any way. He didn't trust the sword, she could tell, but he also wasn't going to throw away a possible solution just because he didn't like it. Not yet. But, oh, how he didn't like it!

Bells couldn't blame him, though. She sensed the sword was unhappy with Jaekob carrying it, but if not him, then who? Assuming the old legends were right, the sword was destined to be with someone mighty enough to save the world. She couldn't get rid of it for no good reason, especially after all they'd gone through to get it in the first place. If Jaekob had actually thrown it, she told him after they landed, then she would have done everything in her limited power to force him to go back and let her get it. When he'd pointed out it would do a fae very little good, she hadn't cared. She would have carried it to the Sword Society who sent them, at the very least.

"Someone's destiny is with that sword," she muttered, not meaning to say it aloud.

"So you've said. Are you trying to convince me or yourself? I'm telling you, this isn't the solution to our problem. I wish you'd believe me."

Actually, she didn't believe him at all. She had the opposite feeling. She felt deep inside that this sword would solve their problems. She felt it strongly enough that she would have jumped off his back to get the sword back if he had thrown it mid-air. She'd have had to trust him not to let her fall to her death.

The next morning, they rose early and flew to the city, stopping just outside the city line because the number of flying dragon squads on air patrol was even greater than when they'd left. They had to walk in. Secretly, she was happy to do it. Dragons must have magically reinforced the Wards even more while she and Jaekob had been gone, and without knowing just what they'd done to it, flying across that threshold seemed like a very bad idea.

They walked the last quarter-mile into the city. Everything was eerily quiet, but they were in the city less than ten minutes when that silence was shattered. East of them, her extended senses heard what sounded like a fight.

"Jaekob," she said, pointing to the east. "I hear a battle ahead. The city is so quiet, who could be fighting?"

"Follow me and stay close," Jaekob growled. He ran toward the sounds of battle with Bells right behind him. A couple of minutes later, he skidded to a halt and said, "I see them ahead."

Bells could already hear the terrible sounds of fighting, even without casting her senses ahead of them. When she nodded, he bolted away and she ran after him. They went a block west, and when they crossed a major intersection, the sounds shifted to just north of them. The city buildings played tricks on loud noises, she realized, sounds bouncing around in the artificial canyons.

They rounded the corner and once again froze in place, this time spotting it at the same time—two packs of weres were fighting each other, and Bells recognized the big one who had declared his loyalty to Jaekob. She hissed at Jaekob, "You sent them here. This is our responsibility. We have to split them up before more get hurt."

Jaekob nodded, his face grim. Bells got the impression that he would have let them be if she hadn't been there insisting he help. He drew the sword and said under his breath, "A dragon takes care of his responsibilities."

He charged forward toward the massive melee, and Bells felt a kind of concern for him she hadn't felt before.

Bells chased after Jaekob as he ran toward the fray. Two werewolves had tussled but were separating to circle one another. Both packs stood in two parallel lines only ten feet apart, growling at each other and barking. Some shouted threats in wolfish, growling voices. Both the Alphas facing each other bled from deep scratches, but the wounds were light enough that both healed quickly, despite being caused by werewolf claws and fangs. Everyone knew those healed slowly—if at all.

Bells shouted, "Stop, stop fighting! What is going on here?"

Neither Alpha nor their packmembers paid her any attention. The two Alphas crashed into each other again, then separated. New slashes in both bled a little but were healing before Bells' eyes.

Jaekob said, "Who dares fight a battle in my city? The dragons rule here, not weres." He had the sword drawn, and again, the runes glowed brightly.

The Alpha who had sworn his pack to Jaekob glanced at him but kept at the ready. He shifted from an offensive stance to one that looked to Bells to be defensive, though she couldn't be sure. He growled, "My prince, we didn't mean to offend you. The Bloody Fangs are here, where I knew you would be traveling. I won't allow a threat to your life."

Bells noticed Jaekob didn't get between the two lines and breathed a sigh of relief. Still, twenty-four weres could rip even a dragon apart, despite his scales and dragonfire.

The other Alpha spat blood. "What do I care if a dragon passes through his own city? You've lost your mind. All of you Throat Ripper pups are crazy. What makes you think you can tell a free were they can't go where they want, do what they want? Are you *my* pack's leader?"

"I will be if you keep talking," the black-furred Alpha roared.

"Stop! Now!" Jaekob roared. "We have enough problems without Werewolves marking each other's trees."

Bells' eyes went wide as she watched the weres relax, men and women alike. Claws retracted, and some sat on their haunches, panting. That was *not* the behavior she expected from weres facing off over territory. They weren't evil, but they were violent and bloody by nature. And when two packs met, everyone knew they didn't stop until one surrendered to the other. Werewolves were pack animals in their souls. "Jaekob—"

"I see it," he replied. He didn't take his eyes off the two Alphas, who now stood only feet apart, neither showing any sign of aggression.

The first Alpha said, "We're sorry, Prince of Dragons. I took it upon myself to make sure your territory was safe for you to pass through."

The new Alpha nodded. "That makes sense, but we're no threat to you."

Bells couldn't believe her ears. None of it made sense.

Jaekob said, "You're in my city, and you'll obey me. There will be no fighting here, today. We need people fighting the infection, not other Pures."

The new Alpha summoned his human form and Bells again felt revulsion at the wet, tearing sounds it made as he transformed. Then he sank to one knee, head lowered. "Prince of Dragons, my pack and I serve your will. I swear my loyalty to you, now and always."

Jaekob did a double-take, then stood up straighter and let the sword's tip droop low. He glanced at Bells, eyebrow raised.

She shrugged, having no idea why they were acting so strangely. "Any idea what's going on?" she whispered.

Jaekob pursed his lips and nodded. "I have an idea, yeah. This sword is a menace, that's what."

"Maybe that's how it is supposed to save the world. By keeping people from wanting to fight."

His eyes narrowed for a moment. Softly, he said, "By taking away their will? Never. We have to find a way to hide this cursed sword before someone dangerous gets their hands on it."

Bells stared at him with her mouth open in shock. How could he still think that after stopping two packs from ripping into each other? How could it be bad to make people peaceful like the fae?

He raised his eyebrow. "You don't like the idea?" he whispered. "I get it. I don't, either, but I like it better than bringing peace by enchanting everyone and making them into willing slaves. You're almost a slave, Bells, so I don't understand how you could want that for everyone on Earth... I don't think you do, though."

She tried to think of something to change his mind but couldn't. Taking people's free will was beyond wrong, as fae knew better than most. She glanced at the two werewolf packs, now Jaekob's loyal, passive troops, and shuddered. Weres weren't passive, and they didn't give their loyalty to someone outside the pack without even a fight.

Suddenly, she was as afraid of that sword as Jaekob was. Enslaving people wasn't much better than killing them. "Well, you're the Dragon Prince. Maybe you're right and we should hide it so no one else can use it."

The two werewolf packs lounged together several yards away as Bells and Jaekob discussed what to do with the sword. "No," she said, "we can't just dump it in the harbor. The mermaids would find it eventually, and you know how they are."

Jaekob's lip curled back into a snarl. Everyone knew how mermaids were. "Fine, then what about taking it to Mount Rainier? All that lava and the destroyed Warrens make it a good place to hide something."

"Except that people will figure out where you hid it. We figured out which one it was in, and they could, too. I'm not certain this sword would even burn up in lava, and someone could figure out how to retrieve it."

Jaekob growled, a rumble from deep in his chest. Then he took a deep breath and forced a smile. "Okay. So, do you have any ideas where to hide this Pandora's Box of a sword?"

She blinked rapidly. He was asking her? A mere fae. Surprised and uncomfortable, her cheeks flushed red and hot. "Well, yes, actually. I only know of one place this side of the Veil where only dragons can enter, and it's a place dragons aren't going back to anytime soon. The Warrens. Safeholme, actually."

"So, okay, that's funny. Now, how about a serious answer? This is a serious problem." Jaekob wrinkled his nose.

"I am being serious. No Pures can get in there except dragons, and none of your people have any reason or desire to go back down there any time soon. I know you all have reinforced the Wards in Safeholme even more than you have in Philadelphia, right?"

Jaekob shook his head and sighed. "Yeah, they have no desire to go down there. Neither do I. Can't we just drop it in a volcano? This thing can't be trusted."

"What if we do end up needing it to save the world? You should hide it, not destroy it. And as I said, that's not a guaranteed solution." Bells stared into his eyes, willing him to go with her Warrens idea.

"Then can't we just bury it in the middle of the Sahara desert?" Jaekob made a fist with one hand and then rested his head on it, drumming his fingers on his leg with the other hand.

Bells fought back a burst of laughter and he frowned at her. She said, "I'm sorry, I'm not laughing at you."

"Just my idea?" He smiled wanly.

"Yes. This thing is so powerful that anyone scrying for it will find it unless it's behind your Wards. Few know about it anyway, but at least the six people we heard it from do, and Creation only knows who else. At least one other group, the Sword

Society's enemies. They mentioned them in passing."

He leaped up from his seat and clapped his hands together. "Right. Okay, then, it's the Warrens. Let's get moving."

"Right now?" Bells climbed to her feet, as well.

"This sword doesn't like me. Maybe it's because I have no interest in using it to dominate people. Since it doesn't want to be very useful to me, it's not going to help us stop the people behind this infection and it's far too dangerous to leave alone for even a moment."

That was an understatement. "Fine, let's go. I know this thing could solve the big problem but it might cause another one just as bad. The faster we get it hidden, the faster we can get back to fighting the infection." She respected him for not wanting to dominate others but it was frustrating to have the solution in their hands and not use it.

Jaekob looked at her intently. After a moment, he smiled and said, "I'm sorry, I just can't take people's will away, enslaving them. I'll never be a slave master, I swear it on my honor. It's unfortunate that it makes saving the world harder, but there must be another way. A better way."

She nodded, forcing a smile as she realized he wanted to be reassured that he was making the right choice. The only problem was that she wasn't sure of it at all. And yet, if he had rushed to dominate everyone in his path, she'd have lost all respect for him. Not that the opinion of a fae mattered to any Pures, especially not to dragons. "Off we go, then. Can't fly out. Are we driving?"

Jaekob's eyes went wide. "No way. It would draw far too much attention. We want to be ignored, not remembered. We'll have to ride out to the Warrens entrance by your village, if I remember right."

"I don't know how to ride," Bells cried. Embarrassed, she added, "The elves never let us." When did slaves get to ride horses, after all?

They couldn't fly, couldn't drive, couldn't ride. They would just have to walk. She'd done it before, when she came to the city in the first place.

Jaekob saw her expression and laughed, pointing at her. Gasping for breath, he said, "Sorry. You should see your expression. I guess you're in for a treat, then, because there's no choice. We have to ride. If you can't do it, then you can sit on my horse in front of me where I can make sure you don't fall off. I'll bring an extra horse for when you get more comfortable on them."

"If I never get comfortable on one? Those things are *huge* compared to me." At only five feet tall, fae were miniscule beside those monstrous beasts.

Jaekob smirked. "Then the extra horse will be for when the first one who gets tired of carrying all that extra weight."

She felt a flash of fire in her gut, hot anger rising. First, he didn't want to fight to free fellow Pures who were virtual slaves, and now, he didn't want to walk. His high-and-mighty feet must be too tender for—gasp!—walking. And he was a jerk for commenting on her weight. She looked down, frowning. She'd never seen herself as being overweight, before. She thought of herself as pleasantly curvy. Fae worked hard to survive, after all, so they were fit. But now, she wondered if she'd been deluded. Maybe it was all the barley fae ate...

Well, fine. If he was going to be like that, while she might have to go with him to save both worlds, she didn't have to talk to a rude dragon. Part of her knew her silence wouldn't last long, as fae simply *did not* ignore other Pures, but the idea of it felt absolutely great at the moment.

She followed him toward the stables, silent and lost in her own thoughts.

J.A. Culican

The exciting rush from her first time riding a horse wore off quickly; her quickened heartbeat lasted much longer, but then again, she had Jaekob's strong arms around her to hold her up in the saddle. He was rude and selfish, which wasn't surprising from the heir to the First Councilor, but he was as attractive as he probably knew he was. She felt a twinge of guilt at enjoying the experience. It wasn't every day that a fae had a Dragon Prince's arms around her.

Behind them stretched two werewolf packs running in parallel rows. Jaekob had told them to get behind him and they'd gladly obeyed. It was comforting to know she had a virtual army of weres at her back, even if they were only there because of something truly horrible. Maybe they'd leave of their own free will after she and Jaekob hid the sword. She hoped so.

A giant insect buzzed past her face, so fast that it was just a blur. Her gaze naturally followed it and she saw the thing strike dirt, then skip twice before stopping, embedded in a soft pine tree. That was no insect. It was an arrow—

"Ambush!" Jaekob cried at the same time she saw it. From the ridges along both sides of the road, elves and trolls leaped toward them, sliding down the embankments with their weapons drawn. It was no welcoming party.

Jaekob dismounted, taking Bells with him and not gently. They were just in time to get off the horse before it reared and then bolted away. As she climbed to her feet, pulling out a knife, the two werewolf packs caught up and rushed the oncoming attackers, howling furiously. Only a second later, she heard a troll scream and a wolf howled in agony.

Then everything went crazy. Blood and chaos—that was the only way she could have described it. Dozens of elves and trolls rushed down the embankments, their downhill momentum allowing them to crash into the werewolves and knock them aside. They kept right on coming toward her and Jaekob. While the werewolves killed some elves and trolls, they weren't killing fast enough to make it worth the losses they, too, sustained. She and Jaekob's followers were too outnumbered.

Jaekob used his arm as a bar across her chest and pushed her behind him as he drew the Sword of Fire. The runes pulsed once, then lit up as brightly as the sun; she could hardly look at it. Bells instinctively used Jaekob's shadow, cast by the sword's light, to vanish into her shadow-walk, a fae's best hope of survival.

Unaware that she had vanished, Jaekob raised the sword above his head and the battle slowed as people on both sides turned, mesmerized by the sword and its lights.

Bells once again thought he looked every bit the mythological hero from old stories...

His military-trained voice rose above the screams and clanks of weapons striking claws, fangs rending helmets, as he cried out. "Hold! You dare raise a blade against the heir to the First Councilor, lord of dragons? I command you," he shouted, and the sword runes flared brighter, "if you want to live to see your families, then put down your—"

Thunk. Thunk. Thunk. Three arrows impaled Jaekob at the same moment, two in his back and one in his chest. He jerked hard as each one struck and the ancient sword flew from his hand when the last arrow pierced his heart. Then he fell to one side like a tree toppling, landing in the dirt with a thud.

Bells grabbed her own face with both hands and screamed in horror as Jaekob stopped and looked down at the arrow sticking out of his chest. He looked confused, but she was confused, too. How could simple arrows punch through his dragon scales? She had seen him take far worse blows and simply shrug them off, so this couldn't be happening. It wasn't possible.

Her stomach flipped as she realized he hadn't actually seen the arrows coming. Was that important? She had no way of knowing. They could have been enchanted arrows, it dawned on her, and if they were, then it meant this was an assassination attempt, not some random banditry in the middle of a chaotic situation in the city.

With her shadow gone, Bells vaulted away, back-flipping to the sword. It had to be kept safe. As she flipped, she caught tumbling glimpses of two elves sprinting toward her, and her fear made her move even faster.

There, the sword! As she landed on her hands, she snatched it up. She was stunned when the sword's grip felt warm and sent tingles through her hand. As she brought her feet up over her head, not slowing down, she again looked for the oncoming elves. One stood only two feet from her and was already swinging a heavy mace. Frantic, Bells used her energy to thicken the air between them, but the mace was faster. Her spell only slowed it down a fraction before it was through her feeble shield.

The mace struck her in her gut and pain rocketed through her whole body. Agony pierced her ribs, as well, and she knew immediately that at least a couple ribs had broken. The force lifted her off the ground and sent her flying in one direction, the dislodged sword in another.

She landed in a building's shadow and used her ability even before her slide came to a halt. She rolled away from where she landed as the elf smashed his mace into the ground she'd just been lying on. She froze, covering her mouth and trying not to breathe loudly from pain and exertion. Her only hope was to go unnoticed.

The elf swung his mace to his left and his right, one missing her by inches, the other by feet. He snarled a curse, then backed away from the shadow. He got a few paces safely away from the shadow he knew must be hiding a fae, then he bolted toward the sword and snatched it up.

When he held it over his head, face twisted into a triumphant snarl, the fighting stopped in seconds—the elves and Jaekob's werewolf packs both halting mid-swing to turn to the elf bearing the sword.

Oh no...

The Sword of Fire worked for him, and there was nothing she could do to stop it. If she revealed herself, could she end up its slave? It seemed likely. Her gaze landed on Jaekob lying bloody in the mud and her eyes welled up with tears. She suddenly didn't care at all about his occasional selfishness or that he was the only hope for the fae to be free. In a moment of crystal clear honesty, she realized she just wanted him beside her, alive and well. She was helpless to go to him, though.

The elf wielding the ancient sword shouted, "All who stand with us, rally to me!" The remaining elves, trolls, and even the werewolves all circled him, pressing close and reaching out to touch him. His mouth moved, but he spoke in a low tone and Bells couldn't hear what he said.

It turned out to be a spell. A moment later, violet-colored tendrils of smoke rose up around the group like a hundred writhing snakes, and when the people were wrapped completely in tendrils, they burst into a flash of light with a loud pop. When the light vanished, so had their enemies. The lavender tentacles writhed their way back into the dirt and disappeared.

Bells ran to Jaekob's body, crying out for help, but there was no one around to hear.

All thoughts for her own safety vanished and she sprinted to Jaekob's side. His aura was weak but it was still there—he was alive, though not for long. She paused, her stomach churning, and her options flashed through her mind in a blur. She could run for help but he'd likely be dead before she found anyone.

She could run home and hide, but whoever had that sword wasn't going to keep it in a vault. They were going to use it and her village would probably be one of the first to fall, being close to the city. Plus, the very idea of leaving Jaekob there to die while she ran made her bile rise in her throat. She could never live with herself.

All that remained were her fae powers. But this wasn't like a bruise or small cut. When a fae healed someone, a part of her power went into the other person and they became connected. For a small cut, the difference would never even be noticed, but to save someone's life was a profound choice with real consequences. Fae rarely healed fatal wounds unless the victim was in their immediate family, and sometimes not even then.

She thought through the consequences. If she tried to save him and it worked, they would be joined together, connected by their auras touching. It meant they'd be able to tell each other's moods instinctively, no matter the distance, almost like having someone in her head. If one were wounded, a fraction of the energy they lost would also be lost by the other, like a sudden flu.

Also, he might pick up traits from her, like being more timid, less ruthless, less brave. The opposite was also true. Could she live with that? Could Jaekob? Or, because they weren't the same Pure race, it was possible there would be no shifting traits. There was no way to tell, and in all the legends she'd heard around the hearth growing up, she had never heard of a fae saving a dragon.

She didn't want him knowing how she felt about him, especially when she wasn't even sure how she felt, in fact. But she didn't want him to die, that was the only certain thing. Not only was Jaekob the only one who could or would help get the sword back, but some part of her cared about his fate more than she wanted to admit.

"The sword," she muttered at last. Maybe it was an excuse, but it was a real one. She needed Jaekob to save the world. She began to hum a melody that sounded like an evening forest, a babbling brook; it was as though birds were chirping and the sky was rumbling with a spring thunderstorm at the same time. Some called it a spell, but she didn't believe the fae used magic. No, they used the web of connections that joined everything in the world to every other thing just by bending the threads and weaving something new.

As she hummed, she felt Jaekob's wounds closing around the arrowheads and shafts. She also soothed his aura, unbending it and shifting it from an almost neon red to a gentle pastel blue, sending him into a deep sleep to spare him the pain of what she had to do.

When the internal bleeding stopped, it was time for the brutal part. Still humming, she grabbed one arrow shaft firmly and pulled it out with a strong and steady pressure. The wide heads caused fresh wounds on their way out, but nothing like if she had yanked them out before giving him a lot of healing.

When she withdrew the third and final arrow, she laid her hands over the wound on his chest and her energy flooded into him. There was so much damage, it shocked her that he had survived long enough for her to get to him. One lung was punctured and both were nearly full of blood. A gash ran through his liver, oozing black gore into his body. And the last arrow she removed had struck one kidney, dead-center. She could *feel* the toxins leaking into his bloodstream.

She had to grit her teeth as she hummed, and her whole body shook with the effort. He was healing, but slowly—there was so much damage!—and the longer she kept at it, the more a growing faintness threatened to overtake her. But she would not stop, not while she had a sliver of hope to save his life and with him, the world. Her family was in that world.

At last, the bleeding stopped and the toxins were neutralized; his skin began to knit together where the arrows had cut through twice. She shook, starting to convulse, and her vision faded at the edges. And yet Jaekob still hadn't woken up. She rallied the last of her strength. She had never used so much energy so quickly. She hadn't even known she was capable of it. *Wake up, Jaekob,* she screamed at him in her mind, though her chanting didn't waver. *The world needs you. I... need you.*

Just as her eyes began to roll back into her head, her vision nearly all black, Jaekob coughed. She collapsed to the ground next to him, utterly spent. He coughed again, much harder, and turned his head away from her to spit out a big gob of blood, then another.

Bells could only watch him, knowing he would almost certainly live. His aura was strong again, though hers was so weak it flickered. He rolled onto his belly and struggled to his hands and knees, then had to rest, sitting on his heels as he gasped to catch his breath again.

He looked over at her and did a double-take. His eyes grew wide and began to glow red. "Are you okay? Who did this to you?" he asked, practically shouting.

Good. His strength was returning. Bells smiled weakly and whispered, "I'm fine. I did it. Are you in pain?" If he were, she still had work to do on him, but it would have to wait until she recharged her energy with sleep.

"No, I'm fine. Did you..." His voice trailed off. Then he shook his head. "It doesn't matter. We have to get out of here. Can you walk? Do you need to be carried?"

Bells' heart skipped a beat. No way she was going to let him think she was so weak that he had to carry her, although the idea of his arms lifting her up wasn't entirely without its charms. No, no—she was letting her imagination get in the way of reality. "Thank you, but I think I can walk. I just need a minute to rest." She yawned hard, her eyes scrunched tightly, and it felt like it went on forever.

Then she blinked a few times. She took a deep breath and let it out slowly, then climbed to her feet. She was shaky still but that would go away. She hoped he hadn't noticed her shakiness, but his amused smile told her he had. She felt her cheeks growing warm. "Why do we have to get out of here? The attackers are gone and there's no one around. We're safe."

He shook his head. "What? No, we're not. I don't know why you'd think that. I'm sorry to say, they aren't going to leave the prince's corpse lying on the street. They will definitely send someone back for my body. There is magic the elves could do against my father and my household if they had my body. Plus, I don't want to go with them. Do you?" He grinned.

Bells felt her hands stop shaking at last and pulled them out from behind her back. "Okay, let's get out of here."

He frowned and huffed once. "The weres will track us. I'm in no condition to fly, not yet." He rolled his shoulders but winced, letting out a little grunt.

Bells grinned and he cocked his head, grinning back at her, big and sloppy. "What?" he asked.

"Well, hiding and running is what we fae do best. Don't you worry, I got this." She moved her hands to make a pattern in the air and each time she repeated it, the pattern grew more solid, more visible. It glowed green and red and purple. Her voice pitched higher with each repetition. When the rune grew so bright that she couldn't see through it at all anymore, she put her lips together and blew out, making a *pop!* noise. At the same time, she stopped moving her hands and spread her fingers out as wide as she could. The rune seemed to split in half, each part drifting through the air at one of them. When they made contact, they burst into tiny butterflies that scattered in every direction, quickly gone.

Jaekob smiled. "Pretty show. But how are we going to avoid being chased?"

"Easy," she said with a wink. "Now we smell like flowers and trees. It lasts until we go to sleep, or until the sun sets and rises again."

He slammed his fist into his other hand. "Fantastic! A neat trick, little fae." His smile faded a bit.

She looked at him questioningly. "So, why are you trying hard not to frown all of a sudden?"

"Now we have to find a way to get through the city without getting caught by those elves, who'll be chasing us soon. And don't forget about all the people who probably aren't very fond of dragons right now for trapping them in with the infection. Or simply for not stopping it yet."

"Fine, but where will we go? Do you think the sword is still in the city?"

"I don't know, but there's only one way to find out for sure. We've got to get to Mikah. This is now bigger than you and me. I hate to say this, but he has to be warned."

"He didn't seem to listen to what you had to say when I met him. And it's a fantastical story. Do you think he'll help us now when he wouldn't before?"

Jaekob's expression grew hard and determined. "It's the only way we'll get the sword back before the elves can put it to terrible use. We'll have to convince him. Let's go," he said, and walked east toward his family manor.

Bells smiled at the thought of seeing Chef again, but then, in the distance, she heard wolves howling and a chill ran up her spine. She hurried to catch up. However bad things might get in the future, Jaekob would heal, her energy would return, and they were going to the safest place in the city. Maybe in the world. Nothing could get to them as long as they were under the shell around Jaekob's home. It would buy them time, and that was what they needed most.

Books by J.A. Culican

Novels

The Prince Returns-Keeper of Dragons book 1

The Elven Alliance-Keeper of Dragons book 2

The Mere Treaty-Keeper of Dragons book 3

The Crowns' Accord-Keeper of Dragons book 4

Second Sight-Hollows Ground book 1

Slayer-Dragon Tamer book 1

Warrior-Dragon Tamer book 2

Protector-Dragon Tamer book 3

Short Stories

The Golden Dragon-Keeper of Dragons short story

Jericho-Keeper of Dragons short story

Phoenix-Hollows Ground short story

Savior-Dragon Tamer short story

About the Author

J.A. Culican is a USA Today Bestselling author of the middle grade fantasy series Keeper of Dragons. Her first novel in the fictional series catapulted a trajectory of titles and awards, including top selling author on the USA Today bestsellers list and Amazon, and a rightfully earned spot as an international best seller. Additional accolades include Best Fantasy Book of 2016, Runner-up in Reality Bites Book Awards, and 1st place for Best Coming of Age Book from the Indie book Awards.

J.A. Culican holds a Master's degree in Special Education from Niagara University, in which she has been teaching special education for over 12 years. She is also the president of the autism awareness non-profit Puzzle Peace United. J.A. Culican resides in Southern New Jersey with her husband and four young children.

Contact me

I can't wait to hear from you!

Email:
jaculican@gmail.com

Website:
http://jaculican.com

Facebook Author Page:
https://www.facebook.com/jaculican

Amazon Author Page:
http://amazon.com/author/jaculican

Twitter:
https://twitter.com/jaculican

Instagram:
http://instagram.com/jaculican

Pinterest:
http://pinterest.com/jaculican

Add me on Goodreads here:
https://www.goodreads.com/author/show/15287808.J_
A_Culican